He flung his shirt onto the desert scrub.

'Now name your next command.'

'Take it off,' she instructed, enjoying the heady sensation of having such power over this man. *This* man.

'What?'

'Everything.'

He made his undressing as slow and as deliberate as he could, and Rose was shocked, startled and unbearably aroused. He read the expression in her eyes as the jodhpurs joined the shirt. 'You worry that I am too much of a man for you?'

She laughed in soft delight at the arrogant boast. 'Maybe you worry that I am too much of a woman for you!'

He took one breathless look at her before coming to lie on top of her.

Rose's head fell back. 'Oh! Khalim!'

'You war   gested teasingly.

Sharon Kendrick started story-telling at the age of eleven and has never really stopped. She likes to write fast-paced, feel-good romances with heroes who are so sexy they'll make your toes curl! Born in west London, she now lives in the beautiful city of Winchester— where she can see the cathedral from her window (but only if she stands on tiptoe). She is married to a medical professor—which may explain why her family get more colds than anyone else on the street—and they have two children, Celia and Patrick. Her passions include music, books, cooking and eating—and drifting off into wonderful daydreams while she works out new plots!

Recent titles by the same author:

SEDUCED BY THE BOSS
THE PATERNITY CLAIM
THE UNLIKELY MISTRESS

SURRENDER TO THE SHEIKH

BY
SHARON KENDRICK

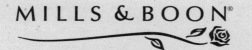

For the debonair Tom Roberts, the world's leading authority on Maraban, and without whom this book would never have been written!

*First published in Great Britain 2001
Harlequin Mills & Boon Limited,
Eton House, 18-24 Paradise Road, Richmond, Surrey TW9 1SR*

© Sharon Kendrick 2001

ISBN 0 263 82518 3

*Set in Times Roman 10¼ on 11¼ pt.
01-0701-52424*

*Printed and bound in Spain
by Litografía Rosés, S.A., Barcelona*

CHAPTER ONE

THERE was something about a wedding. Something magical which made everyday cynicism evaporate into thin air. Rose twisted the stem of her champagne glass thoughtfully as they waited for the best man to begin speaking.

She'd noticed it in the church, where even the most hardened pessimists in the congregation had been busy dabbing away at the corners of their eyes—well, the women, certainly. Women who would normally congregate in wine bars, denouncing the entire male sex as unthinking and uncaring, had been sitting through the entire service with wistful smiles softening their faces beneath the wide-brimmed hats.

Why Rose had even shed a tear herself, and *she* was not a woman given to a public display of emotion!

'In my country,' announced the best man, and his jet-black eyes glittered like ebony as they fixed themselves on the bride and groom, 'we always *begin* the wedding feast with a toast. That their mutual joy shall never be diminished. And so I ask you to raise your glasses and drink to Sabrina and Guy.'

'Sabrina and Guy,' echoed the glittering crowd, and obediently raised their glasses.

Not for the first time, Rose found herself surveying the best man over the top of her glass, along with just about every other female in the room, but then it was hard not to.

He was certainly spectacular—and spectacular in the true sense of the word. But, there again, not many men were fortunate enough to have a real live *prince* acting as their steward!

His name was Prince Khalim, as Sabrina had informed her excitedly when she'd begun to plan the wedding. A real-life

5

prince with a real-life country of his own—the beautiful Maraban—over which he would one day rule, as his forebears had ruled for centuries. He was an old schoolfriend of Guy's, Sabrina had shyly confided to Rose—the two men being as close as two men who'd known each other since childhood could be.

Rose had been expecting the prince to be short and squat and rather ugly—but, for once, her expectations had been way off mark. Because Prince Khalim was quite the most perfect man she had ever set eyes on.

He was tall—though perhaps not quite as tall as the groom—and he wore the most amazing clothes that Rose had ever seen. Exotic clothes in sensual fabrics. An exquisite silken tunic coloured in a soft and creamy gold, with loose trousers worn beneath.

Such an outfit could, Rose reasoned, have made some men look as though they were on their way to a fancy-dress party—maybe even a little bit feminine. But the silk whispered tantalisingly against his flesh, and there was no disguising the lean, hard contours of the body which lay beneath. A body which seemed to exude a raw and vibrant masculinity from every pore.

Rose swallowed, the champagne tasting suddenly bitter in her throat. And then swallowed again as those onyx eyes were levelled in her direction and then narrowed, so that only a night-dark gleam could be seen through the thick, black lashes.

And with a slow and predatory smile, he began to move.

He's coming over, Rose thought, her hands beginning to shake with unfamiliar nerves. He's coming over *here!*

The gloriously dressed women and the morning-suited men parted like waves before him as he made an unhurried approach across the ballroom of the Granchester Hotel, his regal bearing evident with every fluid step that he took. There was a dangerous imperiousness about him which made him the focal point of every eye in the ballroom.

Rose felt her throat constrict with a sudden sense of fear coupled with an even more debilitating desire, and for one mad moment she was tempted to turn around and run from the room. An escape to the powder room! But her legs didn't feel strong enough to carry her, and what would she be running from? she wondered ruefully. Or whom?

And then there was time to think of nothing more, because he had come to a halt in front of her and stood looking down at her, his proud, dark face concealing every emotion other than the one he made no attempt whatsoever to conceal.

Attraction.

Sexual attraction, Rose reminded herself, with a fast-beating heart.

It seemed to emanate from him in almost tangible waves of dark, erotic heat. He wanted to take her to his bed, she recognised faintly, the cruel curve of his mouth and the glint in his black eyes telling her so in no uncertain terms.

'So,' he said softly, in a rich, deep voice. 'Are you aware that you are quite the most beautiful woman at the wedding?'

He sounded so English and it made such an unexpected contrast to those dark, exotic looks, thought Rose. She forced herself to remain steady beneath the dark fire of his stare and shook her head. 'I disagree,' she answered coolly—unbelievably coolly, considering that her heart was racing like a speed-train. 'Don't you know that the bride is always the most beautiful woman at any wedding?'

He turned his head slightly to look at Sabrina in all her wedding finery, so that Rose was given an unrestricted view of the magnificent jut of his jaw and the aquiline curve of his nose.

The voice softened unexpectedly. 'Sabrina?' he murmured. 'Yes, she *is* very beautiful.'

And Rose was unprepared for the sudden vicious wave of jealousy which washed over her. Jealous of *Sabrina*? One of her very best friends? She sucked in a shocked breath.

He turned his head again and once again Rose was caught

full-on in the ebony blaze from his eyes. 'But then so are you—very, very beautiful.' The mouth quirked very slightly as he registered her unsmiling reaction. 'What is the matter? Do you not like compliments?'

'Not from people I barely know!' Rose heard herself saying, with uncharacteristic abruptness.

Only the merest elevation of a jet eyebrow which matched the thick abundance of his black hair gave any indication that he considered her reply offhand. It was clear that people did not speak to him in this way, as a rule.

He gave an almost regretful smile. 'Then you should not dress so fetchingly, should you? You should have covered yourself in something which concealed you from head to foot,' he told her softly, jet eyes moving slowly from the top of her head to the tip of her pink-painted toenails. 'It is all your own fault.'

Even more uncharacteristically, Rose felt colour begin to seep heatedly into her cheeks. She rarely blushed! In her job she dealt with high-powered strangers every single day of her working life, and none of them had had the power to have her standing like this. Like some starstruck adolescent.

'Isn't it?' he prompted, on a sultry murmur.

Rose blinked. She *had* dressed up, yes—but it was a wedding, wasn't it? And every single other woman in the room had gone to town today, just as she had.

A floaty little slip-dress made of sapphire silk-chiffon. The same colour as her eyes, or so the cooing sales assistant had told her. And flirty little sandals with tiny kitten heels. She'd bought those in a stinging pink colour, deliberately *not* matching her dress. But then matching accessories were so passé—even the saleswoman had agreed with that. No hat. She hated confining her thick blonde hair beneath a hat— particularly on a day as hot as this one. Instead, she had ordered a dewy and flamboyant orchid from the nearby florists, in a paler-colour version of the shoes she wore. She'd pinned it into her hair, but she suspected that very soon it would start wilting.

Just as *she* would, if this exotic man continued to subject her to such a calculating, yet lazy look of appraisal.

She decided to put a stop to it right then and there, extending her hand and giving him a friendly-but-slightly-distant smile. 'Rose Thomas,' she said.

He took the hand in his and then looked down at it, and Rose found her eyes hypnotically drawn in the same direction, shocked by her reaction to what she saw. Her skin looked so very white against the dark olive of his and there seemed to be something compellingly erotic about such a distinctive contrast of flesh.

She tried to pull her hand away, but he held tight onto it, and as she drew her indignant gaze upwards it was to find the black eyes fixed on her mockingly.

'And do you know who I am, Rose Thomas?' he questioned silkily.

It was a moment of truth. She could feign ignorance, it was true. But wouldn't a man like this have been up against pretence and insincerity for most of his life?

'Of course I know who you are!' she told him crisply. 'This is the only wedding I've ever been to where a real-life prince has been acting as best man—and I imagine it's the same for most of the other people here, too!'

He smiled, and as she saw the slight relaxation of his body Rose took the opportunity to remove her hand from his.

Khalim felt the stealthy beat of desire as she resisted him. 'What's the matter?' He gave her an expression of mock-reproach. 'Don't you like me touching you, Rose Thomas?'

'Do you *normally* go around touching women you've only just met?' she demanded incredulously. 'Is that a favour which your title confers on you?'

The beat increased as he acknowledged her fire. Resistance was so rarely put in the way of his wishes that it had the effect of increasing them tenfold. He saw the clear blue brilliance of her eyes. No, a hundredfold, he thought and felt his throat thicken.

He gave a shrug. A little-boy look—the black eyes briefly appealing. It was a look that had always worked very well at his English boarding-school, especially with women. 'You took my hand,' he protested. 'You know you did!'

Rose forced a laugh. This was ridiculous! They were sparring over nothing more than a handshake! And Khalim was Guy's friend. Sabrina's friend. She owed it to them to show him a little more courtesy than this. 'Sorry.' She smiled. 'I'm a little overwrought.'

'Is it a man?' he shot out, and before she had time to think about the implications she shook her head.

'What an extraordinary conclusion to jump to!' she protested, but the admonishment made no difference.

'What, then?' he persisted.

'Work, actually,' she said.

'Work?' he demanded, as though she had just said a foreign word.

But then maybe to him it *was* a foreign word. A man like Prince Khalim had probably never had to lift his hand in work. 'Just a busy week.' She shrugged. 'A busy month—a busy year!' She sipped the last of her champagne and gave him a look of question. 'I'm getting myself another one of these—how about you?'

Khalim sucked in a breath of disapproval. How he hated the liberated way of women sometimes! It was not a woman's place to offer a man drinks, and he very nearly told her so, but the fire in her eyes told him that she would simply stalk off if he dared to. And he wanted her far too much to risk that...

'I rarely drink,' he said coolly.

'Good heavens!' said Rose flippantly. 'How does your body get hydrated, then? By intravenous infusion?'

The black eyes narrowed. People didn't make fun of *him*. Women never teased him unless invited to, by him. And never outside the setting of the bedroom. For a moment, he considered stalking away from *her*. But only for a moment. The bright lure of her flaxen hair made him waver as he imagined unpicking it, having it tumble down over his chest—its contrast as marked as when he had pressed his fingers against her soft white skin, just minutes ago.

'Alcohol,' he elaborated tersely.

'Well, I'm sure they run to a few soft drinks,' said Rose. 'But it doesn't matter. I'm going to, anyway. It was nice talking to you, Pr—'

'No!' He caught hold of her wrist, enjoying the purely instinctive dilating of her blue eyes in response to his action, the way her lips fell open into an inviting little 'O'. He imagined the sweet pleasures a mouth like that could work on a man, and had to suppress a shudder of desire. 'Not Prince anything,' he corrected softly. 'I am Khalim. To you.'

She opened her mouth to say something sarcastic, like, Am I supposed to be flattered?—but the ridiculous thing was that she *was* flattered. Absurdly flattered to be told to use his first name. She told herself not to be so stupid, but it didn't seem to work.

'Let me go,' she said breathlessly, but she thrilled at the touch of his skin once more.

'Very well.' He smiled, but this time it was the smile of a man who knew that he had the ability to enslave a woman. 'But only if you agree to come and find me once the music starts, and then we shall dance.'

'Sorry. I never run after a man.'

He could feel the rapid thundering of her pulse beneath his fingertips. 'So you won't?'

The silky voice was nearly as mesmeric as the silky question. 'You'll have to come and find *me*!' she told him recklessly.

He let her go, taking care to conceal his giddy sense of elation. 'Oh, I will,' he said quietly. 'Be very sure of that.' And he watched her go, an idea forming in his mind.

He would make her wait. Make her think that he had changed his mind about dancing. For he knew enough of women to know that his supposed indifference would fan the desire she undoubtedly felt for him. He would tease her with it. Play with her. He knew only too well that anticipation increased the appetite, and thus satisfied the hunger all the more. And Rose Thomas would sigh with thankful pleasure in his arms afterwards.

On still-shaking legs, Rose headed for the bar, hoping that the bewilderment she felt did not show on her face. She did not fall for men like Khalim. She liked subtle, sophisticated and complex men. And while she recognised that he had a keen intelligence—there was also something fundamentally *dangerous* about this black-eyed stranger in his exotic robes.

Inside, she was jelly. *Jelly.* Her hands were trembling by the time she reached the corner of the ballroom where a white-jacketed man tended an assortment of cocktails and champagne.

She could see Sabrina at the far end of the room, a vision in white as she giggled with one of her bridesmaids—Guy's youngest niece.

'Champagne, madam?' smiled the bartender. 'Or a Sea Breeze, perhaps?'

Rose opened her mouth to agree to the former, but changed her mind at the last minute. Because something told her she would need her all her wits about her. And alcohol might just weaken an already weakened guard.

'Just a fizzy water, please,' she said softly.

'Too much of a good thing?' came a voice of dry amusement, and she looked up to find Guy Masters smiling down at her.

Rose liked Sabrina's new husband enormously. He was outrageously handsome, outrageously rich and he loved Sabrina with an intensity which made Rose wistful, and determined that she would never settle for second-best.

Rose had met Sabrina when she had gone in search of a

rare book, and Sabrina had helpfully scoured all the index-files until Rose had found what she'd been looking for. It had been the day after Sabrina had become engaged to Guy, and she had excitedly shown off her ring to Rose—a plain and simple but utterly magnificent diamond.

Sabrina hadn't really known anyone in London, other than Guy's friends, and the two women had been of similar age and similar interests.

'Or are you driving?' questioned Guy, still looking at her glass of mineral water.

'Er, no,' she said, in a faint voice. 'I just want to keep a clear head about me.'

'Quite wise,' remarked Guy, and he lowered his voice by a fraction. 'Since my old friend Khalim seems to have set his sights on you.'

'He...he does?' And then thought how obscenely *star-struck* that sounded. She cleared her throat and fixed a smile onto her lips. 'Not really. We just had a chat, that's all.'

'A *chat*?' asked Guy, now sounding even more amused. 'Khalim exchanging small talk? Now, that'll be a first!'

'Wonderful wedding!' said Rose valiantly, with an urgent need to change the subject. 'Sabrina looks absolutely stunning.

At the mention of his new wife's name, Guy's face softened into a look of tenderness, the intentions of his school-friend instantly forgotten. 'Doesn't she?' he asked indulgently, and then a slight note of impatience entered his voice. 'Between you and me, I just wish we could forget the damned dancing and just *leave*!'

Rose smiled. 'And deny your wife her wedding day! I think you can wait a little longer, don't you, Guy? After all, you've been living together for well over a year now!'

'Yeah,' sighed Guy. 'But this is the first time it will have been, well, legal...' He looked down into Rose's face. 'Why, you're *blushing*!' he observed incredulously. 'I'm sorry, Rose—I certainly didn't mean to embarrass you—'

'No, you weren't. Honestly,' Rose assured him hastily. She wasn't going to point out that it was a pair of glittering jet eyes being lanced provocatively in her direction which had the heat singing remorselessly in her veins. In a way, she wished that maybe Guy and Sabrina *would* leave. And then she could leave, too. And she wouldn't have to dance with Khalim and put herself in what was clearly becoming apparent would be a very vulnerable position indeed.

You don't *have* to dance with him, she reminded herself sternly. It wasn't a royal command. Well, of course it *was*, she realised with a slight edge of disbelief. But even if it was, she was not one of Khalim's subjects and London was not part of his kingdom! She could just give him a small, tight smile and tell him that she wasn't really in the mood for dancing.

Couldn't she?

But in the event she didn't have to. Because Khalim came nowhere near her. She found herself observing him obsessively, while doing her level best not to appear to be doing so.

He stood out from the crowd of fabulously dressed guests, and not by virtue of his own glorious and unconventional attire. No, it went much deeper than that. Rose had never met anyone of royal blood before, and of course she had heard the expression of regal bearing—but up until now she realised that she hadn't really known what it had meant.

There was some innate grace about the way he carried himself. Some fundamental and rare elegance in the way he moved. She had never seen anything like it. People noiselessly slipped from his path. Women stared at him with looks of undisguised and rapacious hunger on their faces.

Did he notice? Rose wondered. His proud, handsome face did not seem to register any emotion at all. But maybe he was used to it. Why, he had only had to lay his hand autocratically on *her* wrist to have her virtually melting at his feet.

The meal was served and Rose found herself seated with a banker on one side of her, and an oceanographer on the other. Both men seemed amusing and intelligent and the oceanographer was handsome in the rugged kind of way which denoted a healthy, outdoor lifestyle. He flirted outrageously with Rose, and even an hour ago she might have been receptive enough to respond.

But the only man who burnt a searing image on her subconscious sat at the top table, picking at his food with the kind of indifference which suggested that conventional hunger was not uppermost in his mind.

At that moment, Khalim looked up and glittered a black look in her direction—a look which sent a shiver tiptoeing down her spine. Quickly, she put her fork down and pushed the plate away.

'So what do you do, Rose?' asked the oceanographer.

She turned to look at him with a smile. 'I'm a head-hunter.'

'Really?' He grinned. 'I guess you earn lots of money, then!'

Which was what people *always* said! 'I wish I did!'

The waitress leaned over, a look of concern on her face. 'Is everything all right with the salmon, miss?'

Rose nodded, looking guiltily at the untouched plate. 'It's fine! I'm just not very hungry, that's all!'

The waitress had the kind of build which suggested that no plate of hers was ever returned unless completely clean. 'Someone in the kitchen just said that we shouldn't bother offering the top table any pudding—so much food has come back from there as well! Maybe you should be sitting with *them*!' she joked.

'Maybe!' laughed Rose politely, half of her thankful that she was nowhere near Khalim, while the other part of her wished desperately to be within his exciting and yet dangerous proximity. She risked another look, seeing how the diamond lights of the chandeliers emphasised the creamy-gold silk of the robes he wore and the raven gleam of his black hair.

Valiantly she forced a few raspberries down her throat, but even the plump and succulent fruit failed to tempt her. And then at last it was time for the cutting of the cake, and the speeches.

Rose could barely take in a word of the best man's speech—she was so mesmerised by his dark, proud face. Her eyes feasted on his features—the hard, bright eyes and the stern expression which made her feel she'd won the lottery when it softened into affection. His mouth was a contrast of lush, sensual curves, but the upper lip had a hard, almost cruel streak. She shivered. Be warned, she thought.

Guy's speech had every woman in the room all misty-eyed with emotion as he gazed down in open adoration at Sabrina and spoke of his love for her.

And then the band struck up and people drifted onto the dance-floor and Rose's heart was in her mouth as she remembered Khalim's intention to dance with her.

But he did not come near her, just returned to his seat and sat there imperiously, his gaze drifting over her from time to time, the black eyes luminous with sensual promise.

Rose allowed herself to dance with whoever asked her, but her heart wasn't in it. She moved mechanically as the oceanographer took her in his arms, stiffening with rejection when he tried to pull her a little closer.

She sat down and was just beginning to seriously hope that Guy and Sabrina would depart for their honeymoon, so that she could leave as well, when Khalim appeared in front of her, the black eyes narrowed in mocking question.

'So,' he said softly. 'I have taken you at your word and come to find you.' The black eyes glittered. 'Though you made yourself very easy to find, Rose—you sweet, blushing flower. Now—' his voice dipped in sultry question '—shall we dance?'

Her cheeks *were* stinging at the implication that she had just been sitting there, waiting for him—but then, *hadn't* she?

'Is that supposed to be an invitation I can't resist?' she shot back at him.

A smile hovered at the edges of his mouth. 'No, Rose,' he purred. 'It is a royal command.'

She opened her mouth to object, but by then it was too late, because he had taken her hand with arrogant assurance and was leading her onto the dance-floor.

'Come,' he said quietly.

She moved into his arms as though her whole life had been a dress rehearsal for that moment. He placed his hands at the slim indentation of her waist, and Rose's fingers drifted with a kind of irresistible inevitability to his shoulders. She breathed in the faint scent of sandalwood about him, its soft muskiness invading her senses with its sweet perfume.

Rose considered herself a modern, independent woman, but a minute in Khalim's embrace was enough to transform her into a woman who felt as helpless as a kitten.

Khalim felt the slow unfurling of desire as he moved his hands down to rest on the slender swell of her hips. 'You dance beautifully, Rose,' he murmured.

'S-so do you,' she managed breathlessly, gloriously aware of the hard, lean body which moved with such innate grace beneath the silken robes. 'L-lovely wedding, wasn't it?' she commented, and said a silent prayer that her sanity would return. And soon!

He didn't reply for a moment. 'All women like weddings,' he mused eventually.

She thought she heard deliberate provocation and lifted her head to stare him straight in the eyes, the bright sapphire of her gaze clashing irrevocably with glittering jet. 'Meaning that men don't, I suppose?'

He raised a mocking brow and thought how bright her hair, and how white her soft skin, against which the soft curves of her lips were a deep, rich pink. Like the roses which bloomed in the gardens of his father's palace and scented the night air with their perfume. His pulse quickened. 'Do you always jump to conclusions, I wonder?'

'But you meant me to,' she parried. 'It was a remark designed to inflame, wasn't it?'

He shook his head, his desire increased by her feisty opposition. 'It was simply an observation,' he demurred. 'Not a…how-do-you-say?' He frowned, as if in deep concentration. 'Ah, yes—a sexist comment!'

Rose leaned away from him a little, and felt the almost imperceptible tightening of his hands on her hips, as though he couldn't bear to let her go. 'You can't pretend to be stumbling over the language with *me*, Khalim!' she said crisply, trying to ignore the thundering of her heart beneath her breast, 'when I happen to know that you went to school in England and are as fluent as I am!'

She was *very* fiery, he thought with a sudden longing. 'And what else do you know about me, Rose Thomas?' he mused.

Briefly she considered affecting total ignorance. This was a man with an ego, that was for sure! Yet how often did people speak their minds to a man with his power and his presence?

'I know that you are the heir to a mountain kingdom—'

'Maraban,' he elaborated softly, and his voice deepened with affectionate pride.

Something imprecise shimmered over her skin at the way he said that single word and a sense of hazy recognition made her shiver. 'Maraban,' she repeated wonderingly, until she realised that she was in danger of sounding starstruck again.

'What else?' he prompted, intrigued by that dreamy look which had softened her features when she had said the name of the land of his birth. And then his mouth hardened. Maraban was an oil-rich country—and didn't fabulous wealth always produce enthusiasm in the greedy hearts of most Westerners?

She wondered what had caused the fleetingly judgemental

look which had hardened his face into a stern mask. She snapped out of her reverie to deliver a few home truths.

'I've heard that you have something of a reputation where women are concerned,' she told him crisply.

'A reputation?' It sounded too close to unaccustomed criticism for Khalim not to experience a sudden flicker of irritation. 'Do elaborate, Rose.'

'Do I need to? You like women, don't you?'

His smile grew cynical. 'And is it wrong to enjoy the many pleasures which the opposite sex can offer?'

His words were accompanied by the splaying of his fingers over her back, and Rose found herself wondering what it would be like if her skin were bare. And his... She swallowed. 'You make women sound like an amusement arcade!'

He smiled. 'It is an interesting analogy,' he remarked, and resisted the urge to move his fingertips to lie just below the jut of her breasts. He wanted her, and he never had to try very hard, not where women were concerned. There had only ever been one woman who had turned him down, and that had been Sabrina.

He moved his head slightly as the bride and groom passed by, and saw Sabrina gazing up into the face of her new husband. Khalim had instantly forgiven and understood her rejection, because she had been in love with his best friend.

Resisting the urge to explore Rose's breasts, he kept his hands right where they were. For while his seduction of Rose Thomas was a certainty, he suspected that he would have to take things slowly...

'So,' he said huskily. 'You are at an advantage, are you not? Since you know something of me, while I know nothing of you, Rose—other than the fact that you are the most beautiful woman in the room.'

'So you said earlier,' answered Rose sweetly, pleased to see the fleeting look of irritation which hardened the dark face. She teased him a little more—just for the hell of it. 'I can't see why women fall for your charms if you keep coming out with the same old compliment!'

'Oh, can't you?' he questioned silkily, and with a fluid movement of grace caught her closer still, so that their bodies melded together with shocking intimacy. He noted with satisfaction the instant darkening of her eyes, the two high spots of colour to her cheeks. Through the thin layers of silk which covered him, and her, he could feel the tiny tight buds of her breasts as they flowered against his chest and he felt another sharp pull of desire.

'D-don't,' protested Rose weakly, shaken by a sweet flood of need, stronger and more powerful than anything she had ever experienced before.

Triumphantly, Khalim felt her tremble against him and pressed his lips close to where the bright, flaxen hair gleamed against her ear. 'Don't what?' he whispered.

'Don't.' But her voice shook so that the word was unrecognisable and she had to try again. 'Don't stand so close to me.'

With the instinctive mastery of the conqueror, he did exactly as she asked, moving a little away from her, and he heard her unmistakable little of gasp of protest. 'Is that better?' he questioned silkily.

Better? Rose felt as bereft as if someone had just shorn off her long hair and left her neck bare and cold. She found herself wanting to beg him to pull her back into that warm, enticing circle, until common sense began to reassert itself. She was not the kind of woman to beg a man to do *anything*. 'Much better,' she agreed levelly.

He didn't believe her for a moment. Khalim smiled, acknowledging what he knew to be a universal truth—that the chase was often the most exciting part of the conquest. 'So why don't you tell me something about yourself?' he murmured.

She turned her face upwards, her eyes sparking a challenge. 'What would you like to know?'

'Everything. Absolutely everything.'

Rose's mouth curved into a smile. 'You'll have to be a *little* more specific than that, I'm afraid!'

He wondered what she would say if he told her the only thing he really wanted to know was what her naked body would look like. Stretched out in rapturous abandon on the slippery-soft sheets of his enormous bed. 'So tell me what you do,' he murmured.

'You mean, work-wise?'

He nodded, thinking that she had no need at all to work. She could easily be a rich man's mistress, he thought. His. Why had he never met her before? 'Or shall I guess what kind of work you do, Rose?'

'You can try!'

'Simple. A model?' he mused.

'I'm not tall enough,' she objected, hating herself for the warm glow which his compliment produced. 'Or thin enough.'

Irresistibly, his eyes were drawn to the luscious swell of breast and hip. 'You are perfect,' he said huskily. 'Quite perfect.'

Within the circle of his arms, Rose shivered. She wasn't *used* to men saying things like that, and certainly not within minutes of meeting her! Mostly, she mixed with lofty intellectuals who might occasionally pay her a clever-clever compliment. Not men who made no attempt to hide a primitive and compelling kind of desire. 'That's outrageous flattery!' she protested.

'Flattery, yes. Outrageous, no!' He turned her round in time with the music, admiring her natural and subtle grace.

He really was the most wonderful dancer, thought Rose. She rarely danced properly like this—and never with a prince! It was heavenly to glide around the dance-floor in the arms of a man. Instead of everyone jigging about doing their own thing and usually managing to connect with her on the way!

He was staring down at her in a thoughtful way, and she immediately wiped the look of dreamy bliss off her face. 'So you've given up, have you? You're not very good at guessing, are you?' she challenged.

'Maybe not, but there are many things I am *extremely* good at, Rose,' he boasted silkily, and chose just that moment to move a silken thigh between hers, immediately losing himself in an erotic dream of making love to her.

In time with the sexual boast, Rose felt the pressure of his leg, and the unmistakable iron of the steely muscle which lay beneath the delicate fabric. An unfamiliar hunger shot through her as she felt her heart-rate soar and something deep inside her began to slowly dissolve. She had to stop this. Now.

'I'm a head-hunter,' she said quickly.

Khalim's dream was shattered by her words. 'Head-hunter?' he questioned, and frowned, his mind firing up with savage imagery.

'Yes, you know—I find people for jobs!'

'I know what a head-hunter is! And you are successful in your line of work?'

'Yes, I am.'

'Then, you must be a very intuitive woman, Rose.' The tip of his finger rippled slowly over the curve of her waist and he felt her shiver in response. 'Ve-ry intuitive.'

Warning bells began ringing in her mind. 'I-I think I've had enough dancing,' she said breathlessly, feeling ridiculously disappointed when he took her at her word and let her go.

'I agree.' The tug of desire had become persistent and uncomfortable. It made him want to take her. To... Khalim found himself having to fight for the rigid self-control which had been a fundamental part of his upbringing. And it was many years since he had had to fight for anything. He took a step backwards, steadying his suddenly shallow breathing.

Missing the feel of silk and the scent of sandalwood, Rose

placed her hands over her flushed cheeks and could feel pulses fluttering absolutely everywhere. And it was only then she noticed that the floor was completely empty and that everyone was standing watching them.

'Oh, my God!' she moaned. 'Look!'

'It seems that we have inadvertently been providing the floor show,' said Khalim, in some amusement, as he followed the direction of her gaze.

Rose's distress grew even more intense, especially as Guy had chosen that moment to approach them and had clearly overheard Khalim's remark.

'A very *erotic* floor show,' he teased.

Rose suppressed a groan. They had been acting like a couple of irresponsible teenagers!

'We were simply dancing.' Khalim shrugged, his black eyes sending out a conspiratorial gleam to Rose.

'Is that what you call it?' joked Guy. 'Anyway, Sabrina and I are planning to leave now.' His grey eyes crinkled as he looked at his best man. 'And thanks for the honeymoon, Khalim.'

Silken shoulders were raised in a careless shrug. 'It is nothing other than my pleasure to give,' he drawled.

'Sabrina told me the destination was a secret,' said Rose.

The two men exchanged glances.

'And so it is. Traditionally, a secret shared between the groom and best man. But do not fear, I will tell you later, beautiful Rose,' promised Khalim softly.

'Later?' she asked, with a quick glance at her wrist-watch. Who had said anything about later?

'But of course. You and I are going for a drink together afterwards.'

Guy smiled. 'Are you?'

Rose saw the black eyes being levelled at her consideringly, saw the arrogant expectation that she would simply fall in with his regal wishes! And who really could blame him, after her shameless display on the dance-floor?

'But you told me you rarely drink, Khalim,' she reminded him innocently. 'So wouldn't that be an awful waste of your time?'

He opened his mouth to object, and then shut it again. Somewhere deep in his groin, Khalim felt a pulse begin to beat with slow insistence. He felt the sweet, sharp tang of desire and yet he instantly recognised her determination to oppose him. It flashed in sapphire sparks from her beautiful blue eyes. No matter what he said, Rose Thomas was not planning on going anywhere with him tonight. 'You don't want to?'

The note of incredulity in his voice was unmistakable, and Rose was very tempted to smile. But something in the cold glitter of his gaze made her decide that smiling maybe wasn't the best idea. 'It's been a long day,' she told him apologetically. 'And I'm bushed! Some other time, perhaps?'

Khalim's face grew distant; indeed, he barely noticed Guy slipping away to find Sabrina. 'I never issue an invitation more than once,' he told her coldly.

Rose was aware of a lurching sense of regret. You've missed your chance, girl, she thought—even while the sane part of her rejoiced. This man was different, she recognised. Different and dangerous. He had the power to make her vulnerable, and he was the last person she wanted to be vulnerable around. Why, a man like that would chew her up and spit her out in little pieces!

'What a pity,' she said lightly.

His black eyes lingered on the lushness of her lips, the creaminess of her skin. 'A pity indeed,' he agreed, briefly bowing his dark head before sweeping away from her across the ballroom.

And she watched him go with a thundering heart.

'They're leaving!' called someone, and Rose looked across the room to see that Sabrina had changed out of her bridal gown into a silvery-blue suit and was carrying her bouquet, Guy in an impressive dark suit at her side.

Everyone began to surge out of the ballroom to wave them off, but Rose hung back. She could see Khalim talking to Guy and she found herself unwilling to face him, aware of a dull sense of an opportunity lost, an opportunity never to be repeated.

She saw Sabrina turn and teasingly hold her bouquet of lilies above her head while every female present lifted their arms in hope of catching it. Even Rose eagerly raised her arms to catch the waxy blooms as they came flying in her direction, but the redhead beside her was more eager still.

'Gotcha!' she shouted as she leapt into the air and pounced triumphantly on the bouquet.

It's only a tradition, Rose told herself dully as she watched the girl ecstatically smelling the flowers. Why would catching a bunch of flowers guarantee that you would be the next to be married? And it wasn't as if she even *wanted* to get married, was it? These days lots and lots of women in their late twenties were electing to stay single.

But when she looked up again, it was to find herself caught in the lancing gaze of a pair of glittering black eyes.

I have to get out of here, she thought, with a sudden sense of panic.

CHAPTER TWO

IN A daze, Rose left the Granchester and found herself a taxi, but afterwards she couldn't recollect a single moment of the journey. Not until the cab drew up outside the flat she shared in Notting Hill did reality begin to seep back into her consciousness as she tried to rid herself of the memory of the dark prince, with his proud, sensual face.

She let herself in through the front door and put her handbag on the hall table, relieved to be home. And safe.

She loved her flat—it was her very first property and occupied the first floor of a grand old high-ceilinged house. But it was an ambitious project for a first-time buyer and the repayments on her loan were high, which was why she had taken on a flatmate—Lara.

Lara was a struggling actress who described herself as Rose's lodger, but Rose never did. Equality was something she strove for in every area of her life. 'No, we're flatmates,' she always insisted.

It was a typical bachelor girls' home—full of colour in the shared areas and rather a lot of chaos in Lara's bedroom— because, much as she nagged, there didn't seem to be anything Rose could do to change Lara's chronic untidiness. So now she had given up trying.

There were brightly coloured scarves floating from a coatstand in the hall, and vases of cheap flowers from the market dotted around the sitting room. And the bathroom was so well stocked with various lotions and potions that it resembled the cosmetics counter of a large department store!

'Anyone at home?' she called.

'I'm in the kitchen!' came the muffled reply, and Rose walked into the kitchen to find Lara busy crunching a chocolate biscuit and pouring coffee into a mug. Her staple diet and *my* coffee, thought Rose ruefully as Lara looked up with a smile and held a second mug up. 'Coffee?'

Rose shook her head. 'No, thanks. I think I need a drink.'

Lara raised her eyebrows in surprise. 'But you've just been to a wedding!'

'And I barely touched a drop all day,' said Rose grimly. She had deliberately avoided liquor so that she would have all her wits about her, and then just look at the way she had behaved on the dance-floor! She sighed as she poured herself a glass of wine from the cask in the fridge.

'Are you okay?' asked Lara curiously.

'Why shouldn't I be?'

'You just seem a little…I don't know…tense.'

Tense? Rose sipped at her wine without enjoyment. She could see her reflection in the pig-shaped mirror which hung on the kitchen wall. Her face was *unbelievably* pale. She looked as if she'd seen a ghost. Or a vision maybe… 'I guess I am,' she said slowly.

'So why? What was the wedding like? Awful?'

'No, beautiful,' said Rose reflectively. 'The most beautiful wedding I've ever been to.'

'Then why the long face?'

Rose sat down at the kitchen table and put her wineglass down heavily. 'It's stupid, really—' She looked up into Lara's frankly interested brown eyes. 'Did I ever tell you that Sabrina's new husband is best friends with a prince?'

Lara's eyes grew larger. 'You're winding me up, right?'

Rose shook her head and bit back a half-smile. It did sound a bit far-fetched. 'No, I'm not. It's the truth. He's prince of a country—more a principality, really—called Maraban—it's in the Middle East.'

'And next, I suppose you'll be telling me that he's outrageously good-looking and rich, to boot!'

Rose sighed. 'Yes! He's exactly that. Just about the most

perfect man you've ever seen. Tall, and dark and handsome—'

'Oh, ha, ha, ha!'

'No, he *is*! Honestly. He's divine. I danced with him…'
Her voice tailed off as she remembered how it felt to have
his body so tantalisingly close to hers. 'Danced with him,
and—'

'And what?'

'And—' No need to point out that she had got a little
carried away on the dance-floor. She squirmed with remembered pleasure and glanced up to see Lara's open-mouthed
expression.

'Oh, Rose, you *didn't*?'

Rose blinked as the implication behind Lara's question
squeaked its way home. 'No, of course I didn't! You surely
don't imagine that I'd meet a man at a wedding and hours
later leap into bed with him, do you?' she questioned indignantly.

But you did it in thought if not in deed, didn't you?
mocked the guilty voice of her conscience.

Lara was looking at her patiently. 'So what happened?'

'He, well, he asked me to go for a drink with him once
the bride and groom had left,' explained Rose.

'What's the problem with that? You said yes, of course?'

'Actually,' said Rose, in a high, forced voice, not quite
believing that she had had the strength of will to go through
with it, 'I said no.'

Lara was blinking at her in bemusement. 'You've lost me!
He's gorgeous, he's royal and you *turned him down*! *Why*,
for heaven's sake?'

'I don't know.' Rose sighed again. 'Well, maybe that's not
true, I suppose I do, really. He's so utterly irresistible—'

'That's usually considered a plus where men are concerned, isn't it?'

'But he would never commit, I know he wouldn't—it's
written all over his face!'

Lara stared at her incredulously. 'Never *commit*?' she echoed. 'I can't believe I'm hearing this! Rose, you've danced with the guy once and already you're talking commitment? And this from the woman who has always vowed never to get married—'

'Until I'm at least thirty-five,' said Rose with a look of fierce determination. 'I'll have achieved something by then, so I'll be ready! And people live longer these days—it makes sense to put off getting married for as long as possible.'

'Very romantic,' said Lara.

'Very realistic,' commented Rose drily.

'So why the talk of commitment—or, rather, the lack of it?'

Rose took a thoughtful sip of wine. She wasn't really sure herself. Maybe because she didn't want to be just another woman in a long line of discarded women.

But wouldn't it just sound fanciful if she told Lara that Khalim had a dangerous power about him which both attracted and yet repelled her? And wouldn't it sound weak if she expressed the very real fear that he could break her heart into smithereens? Lara would quite rightly say that she didn't know him—but Rose was intuitive, more so than usual where Khalim was concerned. She knew that with a bone-deep certainty—she just didn't know why.

She had been 'in love' just twice in her life. A university affair which had occupied her middle year there and then, in her early days in advertising recruitment—she'd dated an account executive for nine fairly blissful months. Until she had discovered one evening that he wasn't really into monogamy.

She wasn't sure whether it was her pride which had been hurt more than anything else, but from that day on she had been sensible and circumspect where men were concerned. She could take them or leave them. And mostly she could leave them...

'Do you fancy going to see a film?' asked Lara, with a glance at the kitchen clock. 'There's still time.'

Rose shook her head. What would be the point of going to a film if you knew for a fact that you wouldn't be able to concentrate on anything other than the most enigmatic face you had ever set eyes on? 'No, thanks. I think I'll take a shower,' she said with a yawn.

Aware that he was being closely watched by his emissary, Khalim paced up and down the penthouse suite with all the stealth and power of a sleek jungle cat. Outside the lights of the city glittered like some fabulous galaxy, but Khalim was impervious to its beauty.

Whenever he was in London on business, which he usually arranged to coincide with Maraban's most inhospitable weather—Khalim always stayed at the Granchester Hotel. He kept the luxurious rooms permanently booked in his name, though for much of the year they lay empty. They had been decorated according to his taste in a way which was as unlike his home in Maraban as it was possible to imagine. Lots of pale, wooden furniture and abstract modern paintings. But that was how he liked to live his life—the contrast between the East and the West each feeding two very different sides of his nature.

Once again, black eyes stared unseeingly out at the blaze of lights which pierced the night sky of London.

Eventually, he turned to Philip Caprice and held the palms of his hands out in a gesture which was a mixture of frustration and disbelief. He'd been bewitched by a pair of dazzling eyes so blue and hair so pale and blonde that he couldn't shake her image from his mind. He had wanted her here with him tonight—on his bed and beneath his body. And he would fill her. Fill her and fill her and…he gave a groan and Philip Caprice looked at him in concern.

'Sir?' he murmured. 'Is something the matter?'

'I cannot believe it!' Khalim stated bluntly and gave a low laugh. 'I must be losing my touch!'

Philip smiled, but said nothing. It was not his place to offer an opinion. His role was to act as a sounding-board for the prince—unless specifically invited to do otherwise.

Khalim turned hectic black eyes towards his emissary, trying to forget her pale enchantment. He could feel the fever of desire heating his blood, making it sing like a siren as it coursed its way around his veins. 'You are not saying anything, Philip!'

'You wish me to?'

Khalim drew a deep breath, swamping down the unfamiliar feeling of having been thwarted. 'Of course,' he said coolly, and then saw Philip's look of indecision. 'By the mane of Akhal-Teke, Philip!' he swore softly. 'Do you think my arrogance so great, my ego so mighty, that I cannot bear to hear the truth from you?'

Philip raised his dark eyebrows. 'Or my interpretation of the truth, sir? Every man's truth is different.'

Khalim smiled. 'Indeed it is. You sound like a true Marabanesh, when you speak like that! Give me your interpretation, Philip. Why have I failed with this woman, where never I have failed before?'

Philip intertwined his long fingers and spoke thoughtfully. 'All your life you have had your every wish pandered to, sir.'

'Not all.' Khalim's eyes narrowed dangerously as he mouthed the soft denial. 'I learnt the rigours of life through an English boarding-school!'

'Yes,' said Philip patiently. 'But ever since you reached manhood, little has been denied to you, sir, you know that very well.' He paused. 'Particularly where women are concerned.'

Khalim expelled a long, slow breath. Was he simply tantalised because for once something had eluded him? Why, some of the most beautiful women in the world had offered themselves to him, but his appetite had always been jaded by what came too easily. 'Only one other woman has ever turned me down before,' he mused.

'Sabrina?' said Philip softly.

Khalim nodded, remembering his easy acceptance of *that*. He tried to work out what was different this time. 'But that was understandable—because she was in love with Guy, and Guy is my friend whom I respect. But this woman…this woman…'

And the attraction had been mutual. She had been fighting her own needs and her own desires, he knew that without a doubt. When he'd taken her in his arms, she'd wanted him with a fire which had matched his own. He'd been certain that he would make love to her tonight, and the unfamiliar taste of disappointment made his mouth taste bitter.

'What is her name?' asked Philip.

'Rose.' The word came out as if it were an integral line of the poetry he had learnt as a child. It sounded as scented-sweet and as petal-soft as the flower itself. But the rose also had a thorn which could draw blood, Khalim reminded himself on a shudder.

'Maybe *she's* in love with someone else?' suggested Philip.

'No.' Khalim shook his head. 'There is no man in her life.'

'She told you that?'

Khalim nodded.

'Maybe she just didn't…' Philip hesitated before saying '…find you attractive?'

Khalim gave an arrogant smile. 'Oh, she did.' He placed his hand over his fast-beating heart. 'She most certainly did,' he murmured, remembering the way she had melted so responsively against his body. And her reaction had not just been about chemistry—undeniable though that had been. No, hers had been a hunger sharpened and defined by the exquisite torture of abstinence.

As his had been. How long since a woman had excited him in this way? Since his father's illness when much of the burden of responsibility for running the country had fallen onto his shoulders, there had been little time to pursue pleasure. And no woman, he realised, had ever excited him in *quite* this way.

Khalim swallowed. Her scent was still clinging to the silk of his robes. Unendurable.

'I must take a bath,' he ground out.

He had a servant draw him up a bath scented with oil of bergamot, and, once alone, he slipped off the silken robes, totally at ease in his nakedness. His body was the colour of deeply polished wood—the muscles honed so that they rippled with true power and strength.

It was a taut and lean body, though he had never stepped inside a gym in his life—that would have been far too narcissistic an occupation for a man like Khalim. But the long, muscular shaft of his thighs bore testimony to hard physical exercise.

Horse-riding was his particular passion, and one of his greatest sources of relaxation. He felt at his most free when riding his beloved Akhal-Teke horse across the salt flats of Maraban with the warm air rushing through his dark hair and the powerful haunches of the stallion clasped tightly between his thighs.

He lay back among the bubbles and let some of the tension soak from his skin, but not all—not by a long way. Rose Thomas and her pale blonde beauty were uppermost in his mind, and thoughts of her brought their own, different kind of tension. He felt the hardening of his body in response to his thoughts, and only through sheer determination of will did he suppress his carnal longing. But then, he had never once lost control over his body...

Should he woo her? he thought carelessly. Besiege her with flowers? Or with jewels perhaps? He rubbed thoughtfully at the darkened shadow of his chin. There wasn't a woman alive who could resist the glittering lure of gems.

He smiled as he stepped from the circular bath and tiny droplets of water gleamed like diamonds on the burnished perfection of his skin.

He had no appetite. Tonight he would work on some of the outstanding government papers he had brought back with him from Maraban.

He slipped on a silken robe in deepest, richest claret and walked barefoot back through the vast sitting room and into the adjoining study, where Philip was busy tapping away at the word processor.

He looked up as Khalim came in.

'Sir?'

'Leave that, now,' ordered Khalim pleasantly. 'I have something else for you.'

'Sir?'

'Find out where Rose Thomas lives. And where she works.'

CHAPTER THREE

EVEN after an hour-long bath and drinking chamomile tea, Rose slept surprisingly little that night. Especially considering that she had had a long and heavy week at work the previous week and then gone out with Sabrina on her 'hen-night' a couple of nights before the wedding.

She tossed and turned for most of the night as an aching sense of regret kept sleep at bay.

And a pair of black eyes kept swimming into her troubled thoughts. Eyes which glittered untold promise, and a body which promised untold pleasure.

She rose late, and was just getting dressed when she heard Lara's voice calling her name excitedly.

'Rose! Quickly!'

'I'll be there in a minute!'

She pulled on an old pair of jeans and a simple pale blue T-shirt and walked into the sitting room, where Lara was clutching excitedly at the most enormous bouquet of flowers she had ever seen.

There were massed blooms of yellow roses, studded with tiny blue cornflowers, and the heady fragrance hit her as soon as she entered the room.

'Wow!' said Rose admiringly. 'Lucky girl! Who's the secret admirer?'

'They aren't for *me*, silly!' choked Lara jealously. 'It's your name on the card—see.'

Her fingers trembling, Rose took the proffered card with a dawning sense of inevitability. She stared down at the envelope, and the distinctive handwriting which spelt out her name.

'Well, aren't you going to open it?' demanded Lara. 'Don't you want to know who they're from?'

'I know exactly who they're from,' said Rose slowly. 'Khalim sent them.'

'You can't know that!'

'Oh, yes, I can.' She gave a wry smile. 'I may have had a few sweet and charming boyfriends, but not one who would spend this much on a bunch of flowers.' But curiosity got the better of her, and she ripped the envelope open to find her hopes and her fears confirmed.

The message was beautifully and arrogantly stark.

'The yellow is for your hair; the blue for the sapphire of your eyes. I will collect you at noon. Khalim.'

'Oh, my *goodness*! How utterly, utterly romantic!' squeaked Lara, who was busy looking over her shoulder.

'You think so?' asked Rose tonelessly.

'Well, I'd be in absolute heaven if I got flowers like these from a man! And what a masterful message! You'd better get a move on!'

But Rose wasn't listening. 'What a *cheek*!' she exploded as her eyes roved over the message again. 'How dare he just *assume* that he can tell me a time and I'll be meekly sitting here waiting, like a lamb to the slaughter?'

'But you aren't going out anywhere else today, are you?' asked Lara in a puzzled voice.

'That isn't the point!'

'Well, what *is* the point?'

'The point is that I don't *want* to go out with him!'

'Don't you? Honestly?'

Honesty was a bit more difficult. Rose had worked hard on her independence and her sense of self-possession—both qualities which she suspected Khalim could vanquish with the ease of a man who had sensual power untold at his fingertips.

'A tiny bit of me does,' she admitted, and saw Lara's face

go all mushy. 'But the rest of me is quite adamant that he would be nothing but bad news!'

Lara sighed. 'So what are you going to do? Tell him that to his face? Or just pretend to be out when he calls?' She brightened a little. '*I* could go instead, if you like!'

Rose was unprepared for the shaft of jealousy which whipped through her with lightning speed. She shook her head. 'I'm a realist,' she said proudly. 'Not a coward. If I turn Khalim down again, then he'll just up the ante—and I am not prepared to be bombarded with charm and expensive trinkets.'

And wouldn't he just wear her down anyway?

'He's the kind of man who thrives on the chase,' she said slowly. 'The kind of man who isn't used to being rejected—it's probably a first for him!'

'So what, then?'

Little shivers of excitement rippled down Rose's spine as a decision formed in her mind. 'I'll go,' she said, in a voice which wasn't quite steady. 'And I'll convince him that I'm not the sort of woman he wants.'

'What sort of woman is that?' asked Lara, mystified.

'A temporary concubine!' said Rose, and then, seeing Lara's expression of mystification grow even deeper, added, 'Someone who will live with him as his wife, until he tires of her, and then on to the next!'

'You don't sound as though you like him very much,' said Lara thoughtfully.

And that was just the trouble. She didn't. And yet she did. Though how could she form *any* kind of opinion about the man, when she didn't really know him at all? She was simply sexually captivated by a man who exuded an animal magnetism which was completely foreign to her.

'I'm going to go and get ready,' she said, looking down at her faded jeans.

'What shall I do with the flowers?'

At the door, Rose turned and smiled. 'I'll forgo the obvious suggestion! You keep them, Lara,' she added kindly, and went back into her bedroom to change.

At least her wardrobe was adequate enough to cope with most things—even something like this. Her job meant that she had to look smart or glamorous whenever the occasion beckoned. Though an outing with a prince was so far outside her experience!

Still, a midday assignation was unlikely to call for much in the way of glitter, and she deliberately chose her most expensive and understated outfit. A demure shirt-dress in chalky-blue linen. It looked very English, she decided, and not in the least bit exotic. As she slid the final button into its hole she wondered whether that was why she had chosen it. To emphasise the differences between her pale restraint and his dark, striking beauty.

She swept her hair back and deftly knotted it into a French plait, and had put on only the barest touch of make-up before she heard the pealing of the front door bell. Drawing in a deep breath for courage and hoping that it might calm the frantic beat of her heart, Rose went out into the hall to answer it.

She pulled open the front door and saw that it was not Khalim who stood there, but a very tall dark-haired man dressed in an immaculate suit, his green eyes glittering with something akin to amusement as he looked down at her belligerent expression.

'Miss Thomas?' he asked smoothly.

He had a cool and rather beautiful face and was the kind of man who might, under normal circumstances, have made her heart beat a little faster. But these were not normal circumstances, Rose reminded herself.

'That's me,' she said inelegantly.

'The Prince Khalim is downstairs waiting for you in the car,' he said quietly. 'Are you ready?'

Rose frowned. 'And you are?'

'My name is Philip Caprice. I am his emissary.'

'Really?' Rose drew her shoulders back. 'And did Prince Khalim not think it *polite* to come and call for me himself?'

Philip Caprice hid a smile. 'It is quite normal for him to send me to collect you.'

'Well, it is not *normal* for me!' said Rose heatedly. 'If he can't even be bothered to get out of the car, then perhaps you would be so kind as to tell him that *I* can't be bothered going downstairs!'

Philip Caprice frowned. 'Look—'

But Rose shook her head. 'I'm sorry,' she said firmly. 'I know you're only doing your job—but your boss's... *invitation*—' she bit the word out sarcastically '—leaves a great deal to be desired. It might have been more polite if he'd actually phoned me to arrange a time, instead of calmly announcing it the way he did! Either he comes up here, or I'm staying put.'

Philip Caprice nodded, his green eyes narrowing, as if recognising determination when he saw it. As if recognising that, on this, she would not be budged.

'I'll go and tell him,' he said. 'Perhaps you could leave the door open?'

'Having to ring the doorbell would be too much of an indignity, I suppose?' she hazarded, but she did as he asked.

She stood for a moment and watched him go, before stalking back into the sitting room where Lara, who had been listening to the entire conversation, was see-sawing between fascination and horror.

'Oh, Rose,' she whispered admiringly. 'You've done it now! Bet you anything he just drives away!'

'I sincerely hope he does,' said Rose coolly.

'Do you really?' came a deep, velvety voice from behind her, and Rose whirled round to see Khalim standing there, with such a glint in his black eyes that she was unable to tell whether he was amused or outraged.

'Y-yes! Yes, I d-do,' she said breathlessly, her heart clenching tightly in her chest as she saw how different he looked today. The eyes glittered with the same predatory promise, but there was not a flowing robe in sight.

Instead he was wearing an exquisitely cut suit in deep charcoal-grey—a modern suit with a mandarin collar which set off the exotic perfection of his face. And where the flowing silk had only hinted at the hard, lean body which lay beneath—the suit left absolutely nothing to the imagination and Rose just couldn't stop looking at him.

His shoulders were broader than she had realised, much broader, while the narrow hips were those of a natural athlete. And the legs…good heavens, those legs seemed to go on forever. Such powerful legs.

Rose opened her mouth to say something, but words just failed her.

'You want me to go away?' he prompted silkily.

Did she? 'It would probably be for the best,' she answered truthfully.

'But you've dressed for lunch,' he observed, his eyes sweeping over the elegance of the pale linen dress.

'Yes, I have.'

'So why waste all that effort?'

'It wasn't much effort.' She shrugged. 'It only took me a few minutes to change!'

'I'm flattered,' he said drily.

She fixed him with a reproving stare. 'I'm used to men being courteous enough to collect their date, and not sending a *servant* to collect them!'

His eyes grew flinty. 'Philip is no servant,' he said coldly. 'He is my emissary.'

'Let's not quibble about terminology!' she returned. 'Why didn't you come yourself?'

Khalim sighed. What would her reaction be if he told her that he had never had to? That all his life he had only had to metaphorically click his fingers and whichever woman he'd wanted would come—if not running, then walking pretty quickly.

'But I am here now,' he said, in as humble an admission as he had ever made. Because he suspected that Rose Thomas was not playing games with him, and that if he pushed her too far then she would simply refuse to come. And he wanted her far too much to even countenance that.

He turned to where a tousled-headed brunette was gazing at him in wonder from the other side of the crimson-painted room, and gave her a slow smile.

'Khalim,' he said, with a slight nod of his head.

Rose was infuriated to see Lara virtually dissolve into a puddle on the carpet—but who could really blame her? It was something outside both their experiences, having a man of this calibre here, exuding vibrancy and sheer physical magnetism.

'L-Lara Black,' she stumbled. 'And I'm very pleased to meet you…K-Khalim.'

Any minute now and her flatmate would start prostrating herself in front of him, thought Rose despairingly. She turned to find those impenetrable dark eyes now fixed on her.

'Shall we go?' he questioned quietly.

She knew that it would be impossible to backtrack, even if she had wanted to—and to her horror she discovered that there was no way she wanted to. She wanted one lunch with this magnificent man. One lunch to show him that she was his equal. That she wouldn't crumble and capitulate in the face of all his undoubted charms.

One lunch, that was all.

'Very well,' she answered, in a quiet tone which matched his.

Khalim very nearly allowed a small smile of triumph to creep onto his lips, until he drew himself up short. There was no victory to be gained from that coolly dispassionate acceptance! he reminded himself. But instead of feeling irritation at her unwillingness to co-operate, he found that his senses were clamouring to life, making his blood sing out that heated, relentless rhythm once more.

'Come, then, Rose,' he said, and gestured for her to precede him.

In the hallway, however, he halted, and Rose's mouth dried as she turned to see why. He was too close. The hall was too small. If she reached out her hand she could touch that proud, beautiful face. Could run her fingertips along his sculpted chin, and meet the faint rasp of shadowed growth there. She swallowed.

Khalim's eyes gleamed. So. He had not been mistaken. It was for her just as it was for him. She wanted him. He noted the coiled-up tension of repressed desire in her rigid frame. He could read it in the dark helplessness of her eyes, and in the fulsome pout of her soft lips.

'So,' he said unsteadily. 'Where would you like to go?'

'Haven't you booked anywhere?' asked Rose in surprise. She had assumed that he would want the best table in one of the best restaurants—and Sunday was traditionally a very busy day for eating out.

'No.' He shook his head.

'That will limit our choice somewhat.'

'I don't think so.' He saw the frown which had creased the milky-white space of skin between two exceptionally fine eyebrows. 'I never have to book,' he explained, and for the first time in his life he realised that he sounded almost apologetic.

And then Rose began to get her first glimmer of the implications of dating this man. She tried to make light of it and smiled. 'One of the perks of being a prince, I suppose?'

'That's right.' He found himself smiling back, unable to resist that sunny and unsettling curve of her mouth. 'Where would you like to go?'

Rose wasn't a head-hunter for nothing. Her 'people skills' were what kept her going in a competitive industry. She guessed that luxury would be second nature to Khalim—so wouldn't he be a little bored with luxury?

'There's a local Italian restaurant called Pronto! on Sutton

Street,' she said. 'Simple food—but good. And you can usually get a table there!'

He was pleasantly surprised, expecting her to plump for somewhere much more up-market than her local restaurant. 'Then let's go and find it,' he murmured.

On the way downstairs, Khalim was hypnotised by the proud set of her shoulders and the plaited hair of brightest gold which had captivated him from the moment he had first seen her.

Outside sat the most luxurious car Rose had ever seen—a great black gleaming monster of a car, with tinted windows and a liveried chauffeur who was standing beside it, and who immediately sprang to open the door.

'Take us to Pronto!,' said Khalim. 'On Sutton Street.' And the chauffeur inclined his head respectfully.

Rose climbed into the back seat, noting that Philip was seated at the front, next to the chauffeur. And next to him, a dark-suited and burly individual. A bodyguard? she wondered nervously. Probably.

The car cruised slowly through the traffic-snarled streets, until it drew up outside a restaurant whose exterior was adorned with a giant picture of the Italian flag.

'Vibrant,' observed Khalim softly as the chauffeur opened the door for them and they both climbed out onto the pavement.

'Isn't Philip joining us?' asked Rose.

Khalim suppressed a feeling very close to frustration, but even closer to jealousy. *Jealousy?* So she wanted his cool and handsome emissary to join them, did she? Was she attracted to him, he wondered in disbelief, or did she simply want a chaperon?

His mouth hardened. 'No, he is not.'

Now, what had put *that* look there? puzzled Rose, shocked by the sudden surge of relief which washed over her. She *wanted* to be on her own with him, she realised sinkingly, her growing attraction to him becoming all too apparent by the moment. But with an effort she managed to shrug it away. 'Fine by me,' she said easily.

Inside the restaurant it was even more vibrant—with Italian music playing gently in the background.

The waitress gave Khalim an appreciative glance. 'Have you booked?' she asked him.

Khalim shook his head. 'Can you fit us in?'

'Sure can!' The waitress grinned, and winked at him.

Rose glanced at Khalim rather nervously. Obviously the woman had no idea that she was being so familiar with a member of Maraban's royal family—but would Khalim be forgiving, or outraged? I don't *care*, she thought fiercely. *I'm* going to enjoy my lunch!

But, strangely, Khalim found that he was enjoying the un-accustomed pleasure of anonymity. Normally he would not sanction such an intimacy—and particularly not from a wait-ress in a rather basic restaurant.

And yet Rose looked incredibly relaxed—even in the cool linen dress which gave her the outward appearance of an ice-maiden—and he wanted to relax *with* her. Not to pull rank.

'Thank you,' he murmured.

Something about the way he spoke made the waitress nar-row her eyes at him, for she suddenly looked rather flustered and led them to what was undoubtedly the best table in the room.

The only one, thought Rose rather wryly, which was not sitting right on top of its neighbours!

He waited until they were seated opposite one another and had been given their menus, before he leaned forward.

'So was this some kind of test, sweet Rose?' he wondered aloud.

She caught the tantalising drift of sandalwood and fought down the desire to let it tug at her senses. 'Test?'

'Mmm.' He looked around. 'Did you think I would baulk at being brought to such spartan surroundings?'

She raised her eyebrows and gave him a considering look.

'Oh, dear me,' she murmured back. 'You may be a prince, but must I also classify you as a snob, Khalim?'

A rebuke was almost unheard of. He could not think of a single other person he would have tolerated it from. But coming from Rose with that quietly mocking tone, it was somehow different. And to Khalim's astonishment, he found himself tacitly accepting it as fair comment.

'You haven't answered my question,' he returned smoothly. '*Was* it some kind of test?'

Why not be honest? Wouldn't a man like this spend his life being told what he *wanted* to hear, rather than the unadulterated truth?

'I thought that you might have had your fill of fancy restaurants,' she observed. 'I mean, surely luxury must grow a little *wearing* if it's relentless? I thought of bringing you to a place you would be least likely to eat in, had the choice of venue been yours. And so I brought you here,' she finished, and lifted her shoulders in a gesture of conciliation.

Guileless! he thought, with unwilling admiration. 'How very perceptive of you, Rose.'

The compliment warmed her far more than it had any right to. 'That's me,' she said flippantly, picking up her menu and beginning to study it, only to glance up and find him studying *her*. 'Shall we order?'

Khalim's black eyes narrowed. He had never had a woman treat him like this! Did she not realise that she should always defer to him? He felt a renewed tension in his body. Strange how such insubordination could fuel his hunger for her even more.

They both ran their eyes over the menus uninterestedly and ordered salads and fish.

'Wine?' questioned Khalim. 'Or would you prefer champagne?'

'But you rarely drink alcohol,' pointed out Rose. She crinkled a smile up at the waitress. 'Just fizzy water, please.'

'Or a fruit punch?' suggested the waitress.

Rose opened her mouth to reply, but Khalim glittered a glance across the table at her, and she shut it obediently.

'Fruit punch,' he agreed, and he began to imagine what it would be like to subdue her in bed.

When they'd been left on their own once more, Rose felt distinctly uncomfortable under his lazy scrutiny.

'Do you *have* to stare at me like that?'

'Like what?' he teased.

As if he would like to slowly remove her dress and run his hands and his lips and his tongue over every centimetre of her body. Rose shivered with excitement. 'You don't need me to spell it out for you. It's insolent.'

'To admire a ravishing woman? Rose, Rose, Rose,' he cajoled softly. 'What kind of men must you have known before me if they did not feast their eyes on such exquisite beauty?'

'Polite ones,' she gritted.

'How very unfortunate for you.' He saw the threat of a glare, and retreated. 'Are we going to spend the whole lunch arguing?'

Arguing seemed a safer bet than feasting her eyes on *him*, though maybe not. Didn't this kind of sparring add yet another frisson to the rapidly building tension between them? Rose felt a slight touch of desperation. Where were her 'people-skills' now, when she most needed them? 'Of course not,' she said, pinning a bright smile to her lips. 'What would you like to talk about?'

She sounded as though she was conducting an interview with him, thought Khalim, with increasing disbelief. By now she should have been eating out of his hand. 'Are you always so…' he chose his word carefully '…*arch* with men?'

'Arch?' Rose took the question seriously. 'You think I'm superior?' Her eyes glinted with amusement. 'Or is it just that you aren't used to women who don't just meekly lie on their backs like a puppy, where you're concerned?'

'Not the best analogy you could have chosen, sweet Rose,' he murmured mockingly. 'Was it?'

And to her horror, Rose started blushing.

He saw the blush. 'My, you *are* very sensitive, aren't you?'

Only with him! 'No.' She shook her head. 'I'm a big girl. I live in the real world. I have a demanding job. If I can't cope with a teasing little comment like that, then I must be losing the plot.' And that was exactly what it felt like. *Losing the plot.* 'Perhaps I *was* being a little arch. Maybe it's a reaction. I just imagine that most women allow you to take the lead, just because of your position.'

'Again, very perceptive,' he mused. 'It makes a refreshing change to have a woman who—'

'Answers back?'

He had been about to say *have a conversation with*, but he allowed Rose her interpretation instead. His own, he realised, would surely have sounded like an omission. What kind of relationships had he had in the past, he wondered, if talking had never been high on the agenda? He nodded. 'If you like.'

The waitress chose that moment to deposit their fruit punches in front of them, and they both took a swift, almost obligatory sip, before putting the glasses down on the table, as if they couldn't wait to be rid of them.

Rose leant forward. 'So where were we?'

Confronted by the pure blue light of her eyes, Khalim felt dazed. He wasn't sure. With an effort, he struggled to regain his thoughts. 'I suspect that it's time to find out a little about one another. One of us asks the questions, while the other provides the answers.'

'Okay.' She nodded, thinking *this* should be interesting. 'Who goes first?' she asked.

By rights, he did. He always did. It was one of the privileges of power. But, perversely, he discovered that he wanted to accede to *her*. 'You do.'

Rose leaned back in her chair. She spent her whole life interviewing people and she knew that the question most often asked was the one which elicited the least imaginative response. So she resisted the desire to ask him what it was *really* like to be a prince. She was beginning to get a pretty good idea for herself. Instead she said, 'Tell me about Maraban.'

Khalim's eyes narrowed. If she had wanted to drive a stake through the very heart of him, she could not have asked a more prescient question. For the land of his birth and his heritage meant more to Khalim than anything else in the world.

'Maraban,' he said, and his voice took on a deep, rich timbre of affection. He smiled almost wistfully. 'If I told you that it was the most beautiful country in the world, would you believe me, Rose?'

When he smiled at her like that, she thought she would have believed just about anything. 'I think I would,' she said slowly, because she could read both passion and possession in his face. 'Tell me about it.'

When he was distracted by the intuitive sapphire sparkle of her eyes, even Maraban seemed like a distant dream, Khalim thought. Did she cast her spell on all men like this?

'It lies at the very heart of the Middle East,' he began slowly, but something in the soft pucker of her lips made the words begin to flow like honey.

Rose listened, mesmerised. His words painted a picture of a magical, faraway place. A land where fig trees and wild walnut trees grew, its mountain slopes covered with forests of juniper and pistachio trees and where dense thickets grew along the riverbanks. He spoke of jackals and wild boar, and the rare pink deer. A place with icy winters and boiling summers. A land of contrasts and rich, stark beauty.

Just like the man sitting opposite her, Rose realised with a start as he stopped speaking. Dazedly she stared down at the table and realised that their meals had been placed in front of them, and had grown cold. She lifted her eyes to meet his, saw the question there.

'It sounds quite beautiful,' she said simply.

He heard the tremor of genuine admiration in her voice. Had he really spoken so frankly to a woman he barely knew? With a sudden air of resolve he gestured towards the untouched food.

'We must eat, if only a little,' he said. 'Or the chef will be offended.'

Rose picked up her fork. She had never felt less like eating in her life—for how could she concentrate on food when this beautiful man with his dark, mobile face made her hungry for something far more basic than food?

'Yes, we must,' she agreed half-heartedly.

They pushed the delicious food around their plates mechanically.

'Tell me about yourself now, Rose,' he instructed softly.

'Essex will sound a little dull after Maraban,' she objected, but he shook his head.

'Tell me.'

She told him all about growing up in a small village, about catching tadpoles in jam-jars and tree-houses and the hammock strung between the two apple trees at the bottom of the garden. About the life-size dolls' house her father had built beside the apple trees for her eighth birthday. 'Just an ordinary life,' she finished.

'Don't ever knock it,' he said drily.

'No.' She looked at him, realising with a sudden rush of insight that an ordinary life would be something always denied to him. And wasn't it human nature to want what you had never had? 'No, I won't.'

'You have brothers and sisters?' Khalim asked suddenly.

She put her fork down, glad for the excuse to. He really *did* seem interested. 'One older brother,' she said. 'No sisters. And you?'

'Two sisters.' He smiled. 'All younger.'

'And a brother?'

'No,' he said flatly. 'No brother.'

'So one day you will inherit Maraban?' she asked, and saw his eyes grew wary.

'Some far-distant day, I pray,' he answered harshly, aware that her question had touched a raw nerve. Reminded him of things he would prefer to forget. Things which simmered irrevocably beneath the surface of his life. His father's health was declining, and the physicians had told him that he would be unlikely to see the year out. The pressure was on to find Khalim a wife.

He stared at the blonde vision sitting opposite him and his mouth hardened. And once he married, then sexual trysts with women such as Rose Thomas would have to stop.

Rose saw the sudden hardening of his features, the new steeliness in his eyes. She shifted back in her seat, knowing that the atmosphere had changed, but not knowing why.

Khalim's breath caught in his throat. Her movement had drawn his attention to the soft swell of her breasts beneath the armoury of her linen dress. She could not have worn anything better designed to conceal her body, he thought, with a hot and mounting frustration—and yet the effect on him was more potent than if she had been clad in clinging Lycra.

In Maraban, the women dressed modestly; it had always been so. Khalim was used to Western women revealing themselves in short skirts or plunging necklines, or jeans which looked as though they had been sprayed on.

But Rose, he realised, had somehow cut a perfectly acceptable middle path. She was decently attired, yet not in the least bit frumpy. Contemporary and chic, and so very, very sexy...

He felt another swift jerk of desire. He must rid himself of this need before it sent him half mad. The sooner he had her, the sooner he could forget her. 'Shall we go?' he asked huskily.

Rose stared at him. The black eyes seemed even blacker, if that was possible, and she knew exactly why. The waves of desire emanating from his sleek physique were almost palpable. Her mouth felt suddenly dry; she knew instinctively what would be next on the agenda. She must resist him. She *must*. He was far too potent. Too attractive by far. Did she want to be just another woman who had fallen into Khalim's bed after a brief glimmer of that imperious smile?

No!

'Why, certainly.' She smiled. 'I have a lot of work back at the flat which needs catching up on.'

He ignored that, even though her offhand attitude inflamed him as much as infuriated him. She would be much more co-operative in a moment or two. He had not misread the signs, of that he was certain.

And Rose Thomas wanted him just as much as he wanted her…

He stood up, and Philip appeared at the door of the restaurant almost immediately.

'Come,' said Khalim.

'Aren't you going to pay the bill?'

'Philip will settle it.'

Rose walked out to the car, where the chauffeur was already opening the door. It was *unbelievable*! Did none of life's tedious little chores ever trouble him? 'I suppose you have someone to do everything for you, do you, Khalim?' she offered drily, then wished she hadn't. For in order to answer her question he had barred her way, and she could see the light of some glorious sexual battle in his eyes.

'I have never exercised my right to have someone bathe me,' he returned softly.

'Your *right*?' she questioned in disbelief. 'To *bathe* you?'

'Why, of course. All princes of Maraban have a master…or mistress of the bathchamber.' He shrugged, enjoying the spontaneous darkening of her eyes, the way her lips were automatically parting. As if waiting for the first thrust of his tongue. Yes, now, he thought. *Now!*

'So where do you want to go from here, Rose?' He dipped his voice into a sultry caress, allowed his mouth to curve with sensual promise. 'Back home to work? Or back to my suite at the Granchester for...coffee?'

His deliberate hesitation left her in no doubt what he *really* had in mind, and as she met the hard glitter of his eyes Rose couldn't deny she was tempted. Well, who wouldn't be? When every pore of that magnificent body just screamed out that Khalim would know everything there was to know about the art of making love and a little bit more besides.

But self-preservation saved her. That, and a sense of pride. One lunch and one arrogant invitation! Did he imagine that would be enough to make her fall eagerly into his bed? She stared into a face which had 'heartbreaker' written all over it.

'Home, please,' she said, and saw a moment of frozen disbelief. 'I have a mountain of work to do.'

CHAPTER FOUR

THE intercom on her desk buzzed and startled Rose out of yet another daydream involving a black-haired man in silken clothes, throwing her down onto a bed and...

'Hel-lo?' she said uncertainly.

'Rose?' came the voice of Rose's boss, Kerry MacColl. 'It's Kerry.'

'Oh, hi, Kerry!'

'Look, something rather exciting has come up and I need to talk to you. Can you come in here for a moment, please?'

'Sure I can.' Trying to project an enthusiasm she definitely wasn't feeling, Rose pushed away the feedback form she had been completing and went out into the corridor towards Kerry's room, which was situated on the other side of the passage.

Headliners was one of London's most successful small head-hunting agencies, and Rose had worked there for two years. It specialised in placing people in jobs within the advertising industry and was famous for its youth, its dynamism and eclectic approach—all highly valued qualities when it came to dealing with their talented, but often temperamental clients!

Their offices were based in Maida Vale, in a charmingly converted mews cottage. It had been deliberately designed so that their workplace seemed more like a home from home, and was the envy of the industry! The theory was that relaxed surroundings helped people do their job better and, so far, the practice was bearing out the theory very nicely.

Rose could see Kerry working at her desk and walked straight in without knocking, since she had always operated an open-door policy. And although, strictly speaking, Kerry

was her boss—she was only a couple of years older than
Rose—she had never found the need to pull rank. Headliners
eight employees all worked as a team, and not a hierarchy.

She looked up as Rose came in, pushed her tinted glasses
back up her nose, and smiled. 'Hi!'

Rose smiled back. 'You wanted to see me?'

Kerry nodded and fixed her with a penetrating look. 'How
are you doing, Rose?'

Rose forced herself to widen her smile. 'Fine.' She nodded. And she was, of course she was. Just because she had
spent the week since her lunch with Khalim thinking about
him during every waking moment—it didn't mean there was
anything wrong with her. And even if when she went to bed
there was no let-up—well, so what? Maybe sleep *didn't* come
easily, and maybe all her dreams *were* invaded by that same
man—but that did not mean she was not fine. She wasn't
sick, or broke, or worried, was she?

She had tried displacement therapy, and thrown herself
into a week of feverish activity. She had spring-cleaned her
bedroom—even though it was almost autumn!—and had
gone to the cinema and the theatre. She had attended the
opening of an avant-garde art exhibition and visited her parents in their rambling old farmhouse.

And still felt as though there was a great, gaping hole in
her life.

'I'm fine,' she said again, wondering if her smile looked
genuine.

Kerry frowned. 'You're quite sure?' she asked gently.
'You've seemed a little off colour this week. A bit pale, too.
And haven't you lost weight?'

For a moment, Rose was tempted to tell her, but she never
bought her problems into work with her. And, anyway, she
didn't *have* a problem! she reminded herself. 'Oh, come on!
Who *isn't* always trying to lose weight?' she joked.

'True.' Kerry indicated the chair opposite her. 'Sit down.'

'Thanks.' Rose wondered what all this was about, and

started to feel the first stirrings of curiosity. Kerry seemed terribly excited about something. And it must be something big because Kerry was the kind of seen-it-all and done-it-all person who wasn't easy to impress.

'What if I told you I'd just had lunch with a client—'

'I'd say lucky you—I just had a boring old sandwich at my desk!' And no need to mention that most of it had ended up in the bin.

'A client.' Kerry sucked in a deep and excited breath and then Rose really *was* surprised. Why, her sophisticated and sometimes cynical boss was looking almost *coquettish*! 'The most surprising and unbelievable client you can imagine.'

'Oh?'

'What would you say if I told you that we are being hired by a—' Kerry gulped the word out as if she couldn't quite believe she was saying it '—*prince*?' Kerry sat back in her chair and looked at Rose, her face a mixture of triumph and curiosity.

Rose felt as though she were taking part in a play. As though someone else had written the script for this scene which was now taking place. It was surely far too much of a coincidence to suppose that…that… Her heart was pounding unevenly in her chest. 'A prince?' she asked weakly, playing for time.

Kerry completely misinterpreted her strangulated words. 'I know,' she confided. 'It took me a little while before I could believe it myself! I mean, there isn't much that surprises *me*, but when a Lawrence-of-Arabia-type character walks into one of London's top restaurants and every woman in the room sat staring at him, open-mouthed. Well, suffice it to say that I was momentarily speechless!'

'That *must* be a first,' said Rose drily, and forced herself to ask the kind of questions she would normally ask if her brain weren't spinning round like a carousel inside her head. 'What did he want?'

'That's the funny thing.' Kerry picked up a pencil and twirled it thoughtfully around in her fingers. 'He wanted *you*.'

Disbelief and a lurching kind of excitement created an unfamiliar cocktail of emotion somewhere deep inside her. *'Me?'* squeaked Rose. 'What do you mean, he wanted me?'

Kerry frowned. 'Calm down, Rose—I'm not talking in the biblical sense!'

No, but you could be sure that *he* was, thought Rose, and her heart-rate rocketed even further.

Kerry smiled encouragingly. 'He—'

'What's his name?' put in Rose quickly, thinking that maybe, just maybe—there *was* another prince in London with dark, exotic looks.

'Khalim,' said Kerry, and her face took on an unusually soft expression. 'Prince Khalim. It's a lovely name, isn't it?'

'Lovely,' echoed Rose faintly. 'Wh-what did you say he wanted?'

'He wants to employ our agency to head-hunt for him! More specifically,' added Kerry, 'he asked especially for *you*.'

'D-do you know why?'

'Oh, yes,' said Kerry happily. 'He told me. Said he'd heard that you were probably the best head-hunter in the city, and that he only ever uses the best!'

The word *uses* swam uncomfortably into her mind and refused to shift. Rose frowned in genuine confusion. 'You mean he's in advertising?'

Kerry shook her head. 'Oh, no—it's nothing to do with advertising. He wants you to find someone to be in charge of his country's oil refinery. The man who has been there since the year dot is taking early retirement, apparently.'

Rose stared across the table in disbelief. 'But we don't *do* oilfields!' she protested. 'Our speciality is advertising.'

'That's exactly what I told him,' said Kerry smugly. 'I felt it was only professional to point that out. I said that my advice would be to consult someone who was familiar with that particular field.'

'And what did he say?' asked Rose, knowing that the question was in many ways redundant, and that she had a good idea of what was coming next.

She had.

'Oh, he said that the principles for finding the right person for the job were the same, no matter what the particular job,' Kerry explained airily. 'Matching skills with needs.'

'I'll bet he did,' said Rose dully. What Khalim wanted, Khalim had to have. And he wanted her, she knew that. The only trouble was that she wanted him, too—and she was only just beginning to discover how much...

Kerry gave her a piercing stare. 'This wasn't the kind of reaction I was expecting, Rose. I thought you'd be leaping up and down with excitement,' she said, and leaned forwards over the desk. 'When someone of this man's stature hears that one of your staff is about the best there is, and decides that no one else will possibly do. Well—' she shrugged, but there was no disguising her disappointment '—*most* people would be absolutely delighted! Is there something you're not telling me?'

Rose was a naturally truthful person, but this was her *boss*. And, anyway, even if she told the truth—how weak and pathetic would she sound if she came straight out with it? Kerry, I've met him and he desires me and I desire him too, but I'm reluctant to start anything that I suspect is only going to end in tears.

'No,' she said quickly. 'There's nothing of any relevance to the job.' And that much was true. If any of her ex-boyfriends had come to the agency requesting that she found someone to work for them—she wouldn't have had a problem doing it. Wasn't she in danger of letting Khalim tangle her life up into knots?

'Think of the opportunities this presents!' enthused Kerry. 'This could give us the chance to branch out into a completely different field. The world could be our oyster—and just think of our profile!'

Kerry spoke sense; the professional in Rose acknowledged that. There was no way she could turn down such a golden opportunity, even if she *had* been railroaded by the coolly manipulative Khalim into doing so. She put as much enthusiasm as she possibly could into her reply. 'I'd love to do it, Kerry.'

Kerry beamed. 'Good! He wants to see you first thing in the morning. Well, ten o'clock, to be precise.'

'Where?' But Rose knew the answer to this, too.

'At his suite. The *penthouse* suite! At the Granchester Hotel.' Kerry winked. '*Very* posh! Just make sure you wear something nice!'

Rose opted for the cover-up. A silk trouser suit in a sugar-almond pink. And the complete opposite of a come-and-get-me look, with her hair caught back in a stark pony-tail and her make-up so sparing that it was virtually non-existent.

She arrived at the Granchester at precisely five to ten and the first person she saw standing at the other end of the vast foyer was Philip Caprice. As expected.

She saw his hand move to the breast pocket of his suit, and then, with a slightly wary smile, he walked across the foyer towards her.

'Hello, Rose.' He smiled.

It wasn't *his* fault that he worked for a man who used his untold influence to control events, she supposed, and she gave him a returning smile.

'Hello, Philip. Khalim sent you down to collect me, I suppose?'

'No, Khalim has come down to fetch you himself,' came a smooth, velvety voice from just behind her, and Rose turned round to find Khalim standing there, the black eyes glittering with some unspoken message. Was that triumph she read there? She supposed it was. He had got exactly what he wanted. Or so he thought...

'And I suppose I should be flattered, should I?' she asked spikily.

Khalim gave a hard smile. 'Actually, yes, perhaps you should. After all, most women find it a pleasure to be in my company.'

'But, presumably, they haven't been manipulated into it, like I have?'

Khalim stilled. 'Are you intending to make a scene in the middle of the foyer?'

'You classify giving a legitimate opinion as making a scene?' Rose smiled. 'What spineless women you must have known in the past, Khalim!'

And looking at the feisty sparkle which was making her blue eyes shine like sapphires, Khalim was inclined to agree with her. 'Shall we go upstairs?' he asked pleasantly.

The words came blurting out before she could stop them. 'Why, so that you can seduce me?'

The black eyes narrowed, but then his mouth curved in a slow, speculative smile. 'Is that what you would like, then, sweet Rose?'

And, to Rose's horror, that smile had the most extraordinary effect on her. She found her skin warming under that unmistakable look of approbation, as if she had found herself beneath the gentle heat of a spring sun. Her heart began to patter out an erratic little dance and little shivers of sensation skittered all the way down her spine.

With a supreme effort, she said firmly, 'No, what I would *like* is to have been given some choice in taking this job!'

'I'm sure you were perfectly free to turn it down.' His shrug was disarming, but the steely intent behind his words remained intact.

'Yes, that would have gone down very well with my boss, wouldn't it? Sorry, but I don't want to take this highly lucrative contract, because...'

'Because?' he questioned so silkily that the hairs on the back of her neck began to prickle, and she stared at him indignantly.

'Because a man who is capable of such underhand—'

But her words were waylaid by long, olive-coloured fingers being placed on her arm. She could feel their gentle caress through the thin silk of her suit jacket, and at that moment felt as helpless as a rabbit caught in the glaring headlights of an oncoming car.

'Let us continue this discussion upstairs,' he instructed smoothly. 'I am not certain that I am going to like what I am about to hear—and, if that is the case, then I most assuredly do not wish for all the staff and guests of the Granchester to be privy to it.'

Rose opened her mouth to protest, then closed it again. What was the point? She was here to do business, after all. 'Will Philip be accompanying us?'

Dark eyebrows were raised in mocking query. 'Ah! Once again you have need of a chaperon do you, Rose?'

Her own look mocked him back. 'Of course not! I'm a professional—and our business will be conducted on just that footing. I know that I can rely on you to abide by that, can't I, Khalim?'

Her attempt to dominate made him ache unbearably, and Khalim felt the slow pull of sexual excitement. What untold pleasure it would give him to subjugate her fiery insurrection!

'A word of warning, Rose,' he murmured. 'A Marabanesh is master of his own destiny. Rely on nothing and you shall not be disappointed.' He turned his dark head. 'Come, Philip,' he drawled. 'The lady requests your company.'

Philip Caprice seemed slightly bemused by the interchange. 'I'm honoured,' he replied.

But Rose could barely think straight. All the way up in the lift, Khalim's words kept swimming seductively around in her head. *Master of his own destiny.* Why should that thrill her so unspeakably? Because the quiet Englishmen of her acquaintance would never have come out with such a passionate and poetic phrase?

His suite was something outside Rose's experience, even though her work had taken her to plenty of glamorous places in her time. But this was something else! She looked around in wonder. It was absolutely vast—why, she could imagine two football teams feeling perfectly at home here! And it was furnished with sumptuous understatement.

She didn't know quite what she had expected—Middle-Eastern opulence, she supposed, with golden swathes of material, and mosaics and richly embroidered cushions scattered on the floor, perhaps even a water-pipe or two!

And she couldn't have got it more wrong, because Khalim's suite was so very English. Comfort, with a slight modern edge to it; it was thickly carpeted in soft pale cream with three enormous sofas coloured blood-red. On the wall hung some magnificent modern paintings—huge canvases whose abstract shapes took the mind on surprising journeys.

But it was the view which was the most stunning thing the suite had to offer—because along the entire length of the room ran floor-to-ceiling windows overlooking London's most famous park. She gazed down, thinking that it was so unexpected to see a great sward of green right bang in the middle of a bustling city.

And when she looked up again, it was to find Khalim watching her.

'You like it,' he observed, and the pleasure in his voice was unmistakable.

'It's beautiful,' she said simply. 'Absolutely beautiful.'

And so was she, he thought. So was she. Quite the most beautiful woman he had ever seen, with her pale blonde hair and milky-white skin, and a pert little nose offset by the most sinful pair of lips imaginable. Again, he felt the irresistible pull of desire, but he quashed it ruthlessly.

At his English boarding-school, he had sometimes liked to fish—the calm and the quiet and the splendid isolation had

soothed his homesick soul during the times he had been missing his homeland quite desperately. And early on he had
learnt that the most prized fish were those which proved the
most difficult to catch.

And so it was with Rose. He acknowledged that she
wanted him, too, and he suspected that she was perceptive
enough to have recognised it herself. But she was not like
other women, he knew that with a blinding certainty. She
would not fall easily into his arms, no matter how much she
wanted him.

He smiled, not oblivious to the impact of that smile.
'Please sit down, Rose. Shall we have coffee?'

His tone was so courteous and his manner so charming
that Rose was momentarily captivated. She completely forgot
about giving him a piece of her mind. Why, for a moment,
she felt almost *flustered*.

'Er, thank you,' she said, and slid down onto one of the
blood-red sofas, astonished when a middle-aged woman, who
was obviously a Marabanesh herself, carried in a tray of
fragrant-smelling coffee.

Had someone been listening for his command? she wondered rather helplessly, before realising that *yes*, they probably had! He *was* a prince, after all, with people hanging
onto his every word.

And then she remembered. He might be a prince, but he
was also a devious manipulator who had used his money and
position and power to get her here today!

With a smile, she took one of the tiny cups from the
woman, and put it down on the floor so that she could delve
into her briefcase.

She extracted a sheaf of papers and fixed him with a bright,
professional smile. 'Right, then. Let's get started!'

'Drink your coffee first.' He frowned.

She gave another brisk smile. 'You're not paying me to
drink coffee, Khalim!'

His frown deepened. 'What do you want to know?' he asked sulkily.

Rose almost smiled again. Why, right then, she got a fleeting glimpse of the little boy he must once have been! And a very handsome little boy, too! 'You went to school with Guy, didn't you?' she asked suddenly.

Satisfied that she had fallen in with his wishes, and was postponing the start of the meeting in deference to him, Khalim nodded. 'A very English boarding-school,' he said and sipped his own coffee.

'How old were you?'

His face suddenly tensed. 'Seven.'

The way he shot that single word out told her it had hurt. And why brush those feelings under the carpet? Wouldn't a prince be 'protected' from so-called prying questions such as those. And if you bottled things up, didn't that mean you would never be able to let them go? 'That must have been very difficult for you,' she ventured cautiously.

Khalim regarded her thoughtfully. Brave, he reasoned. Few would dare to ask him such a personal question, and there were few to whom he would give an answer. But on her angelic face was an expression of genuine concern, not just mere inquisitiveness.

'It wasn't…' He hesitated. A Marabanesh man of his stature would never admit to human frailty. 'Easy,' was all he would allow.

Understatement of the year, thought Rose wryly.

He saw her take her pen out of her briefcase, and suddenly found that he didn't want to talk business. 'It was the tradition,' he said abruptly.

She glanced up. 'The tradition?'

'For princes of Maraban to be educated in England.'

'Why?'

He gave a rather speculative smile and Rose was suddenly alerted to the fact that this man could be ruthless indeed. *Remember* that, she told herself fiercely.

'So that it is possible to blend into both Eastern and Western cultures,' he replied.

And sitting there, with his immaculately cut suit and his handmade Italian shoes, he did indeed look the personification of Western elegance. But the deep olive skin and the glittering black eyes and the decidedly regal bearing bore testament to the fact that his roots were in a hot, scented land which was worlds away from this.

And remember that, *too*, thought Rose.

'Maraban sells oil all over the world,' he continued. 'And wherever I go, I am aware that I am my country's ambassador. It has always been to my advantage that I am able to merge into whichever culture I am with at the time.'

'So you're a chameleon?' asked Rose thoughtfully.

He gave a slow smile. 'I prefer to describe myself as a man of contrasts.'

Hadn't she thought exactly that, the very first time she had met him? Rose shifted uncomfortably. It felt slightly disconcerting, alarming even—to be echoing Khalim's thoughts.

She took a sip from her coffee, then put the cup back down on the floor.

'So, to business. And I need you to tell me, Khalim— exactly what is it you want?' she asked him crisply.

For once it was difficult to focus on business—he couldn't seem to kick-start his mind into gear. He wondered what she would say if he told her that what he *wanted* was to make love to her in such a way that every man who ever followed him would be like a dim memory of the real thing. He felt the powerful thundering of his heart in response to his thoughts.

'Let me give you a little background first,' he began softly. 'Maraban has substantial reserves of oil in—'

'The Asmaln desert,' she put in quickly. 'And other natural resources include deposits of coal, sulphur, magnesium, and salt.'

Khalim looked at her in astonishment. 'And how, for an

Englishwoman, do you know so much about my country?' he demanded.

Rose's mouth pleated with disapproval. 'Oh, *really*, Khalim! Once I knew that I had to take the wretched job, I approached it in exactly the same way as I would any other! Information is power, and I spent until late last night finding out everything I could about Maraban!'

His eyes narrowed with unwilling admiration. 'What else do you know?'

'That only four per cent of the country is cultivated, nearly all of which is irrigated. I also know,' she added, 'that Marabanesh pistachio nuts are considered to be the finest in the world!'

'And do you like pistachio nuts?' he asked seriously.

Her mouth lifted at the corners. 'Oh, I wouldn't dream of having a gin and tonic without one!'

Such flippancy was something he was unused to as well— at least from anyone outside his inner circle. Yet his mouth curved in response to that frankly mischievous smile. 'Then I must arrange to have some sent to you, Rose,' he murmured. 'A whole sackload of Maraban pistachios!'

It was distracting when his hard face softened like that. It started making her imagine all kinds of things. She tried to picture him doing ordinary things. Going to the supermarket. Queuing up at the petrol station. And she couldn't. She tried to picture him on holiday, swimming...

Oddly enough, that was an image which imprinted itself far more clearly and Rose saw glorious dark limbs, all strength and muscle as they submerged themselves in warm and silken waters. With almost painful clarity, she recalled just how it had felt to move within the sandalwood-scented circle of his arms at the wedding reception.

Khalim saw the sudden tension around her shoulders. 'Something is wrong?'

Had he noticed the hectic flush which was burning its way along her cheekbones? She stared fixedly at the pristine papers on her lap, unable to meet his gaze, terrified that his slicing black stare would be able to read the unmistakable longing in her eyes.

'No,' she said, with slow emphasis, until she had composed herself enough to meet that challenging look head-on. 'Nothing is wrong, Khalim. But I'm still waiting for you to tell me what it is you're looking for.'

Khalim recognised her determination, and a will almost as forceful as his own. It was a heady discovery, he thought as he began to speak.

'Maraban has one of the world's most well-run oil refineries and the man who heads it up is taking early retirement.'

'And you want someone to replace him?'

Khalim shook his dark head. 'No one could ever replace Murad,' he said thoughtfully. 'He has been there for many years, and there have been many changes in the industry during that time. No, I need someone to take oil production into the first third of this century and there are two likely candidates working there at present. I need a man with vision to head it up—'

'Or a woman, of course?'

Jet sparks heated the onyx eyes, bathing her in an intensely black light.

'No,' he contradicted resolutely. 'Not a woman. Not in Maraban.'

Rose bristled; she couldn't help herself. She thought about all she had striven to achieve in her life. 'So women aren't equal in Maraban?'

'I think you are intelligent enough to know the answer to that for yourself, without me having to tell you, Rose,' he remonstrated quietly.

'It's disgraceful!' she stormed.

'You think so?' His voice was dangerously soft.

'I know so! Women in this country died to have the right to vote and to call themselves equal!'

'And you think that makes them happy?'

Her eyebrows shot up. 'I can't believe you could even ask me a question like that!'

He smiled, savouring the rare flavour of opposition and conflict. 'I just did.'

Rose very nearly threw her pen across the room in a fit of pique, before remembering herself. Since when had she taken to hurling missiles? She steadied her voice with a deep breath instead. 'Of course equality makes women happy! What woman worth her salt wants to spend her life living in a man's shadow?'

The woman he would marry would be only too glad to. His mind skipped to the women currently being vetted as eligible wife material, then thought how unlike them this woman was. Their very antithesis. He felt the thrill of the forbidden, the lure of the unsuitable, and it heated his blood unbearably. 'You should not judge without all the facts available to you, Rose,' he remonstrated softly. 'Women in Maraban are very highly respected and they are treated with the utmost reverence—because they are seen as the givers of life. Come and see for yourself whether the women of Maraban are happy.'

She stared at him, furiously aware that wild hope was vying with indignation. 'What do you mean?'

In that moment, he had never rejoiced in his position quite so much. How perfect that whatever he desired should be granted to him without effort. And he desired Rose Thomas more than anything in his life to date. He gave a cool and glittering smile. 'You will accompany me to Maraban,' he purred.

CHAPTER FIVE

'YOU *are* kidding, Rose?'

Rose stared at her flatmate, still slightly reeling from Khalim's unarguable statement. 'I wish I was!'

Lara cocked her head to one side and grinned. 'Oh, no, you don't! What other woman do you know who wouldn't want to be whisked off in a private jet with a prince—a *prince*, no less, who looks like Khalim does? And acts like Khalim does!'

'High-handed!' grumbled Rose.

'Masterful,' sighed Lara.

Of course, Lara wasn't entirely wrong—not about Khalim, nor Rose's attitude to being whisked off in such an extraordinary fashion. Because if she examined her feelings honestly, wasn't there a part of her—and quite a large part of her—which was feeling almost sick with excitement at the thought of being taken to Maraban by its overwhelmingly attractive prince and heir? Any minute now she would wake up and find that the alarm had just gone off!

'So tell me why you're going again,' said Lara, screwing her face up, as if she hadn't understood the first explanation, which Rose had blurted out. 'Just to find out about how women in Maraban live, compared to their Western counterparts? Is that it?'

Rose shook her head. 'No. That was just the provocative way he phrased it.' Along with the even more provocative look which had gleamed with such dazzling promise from those inky eyes. 'But the fact is that I'll probably be recruiting from within Maraban itself, or the surrounding countries if that fails. There are two possible candidates there already, so I really do *need* to go.'

'Oh, you poor thing!'

She'd phoned Kerry to broach the subject of her journey, and her boss had sounded bemused.

'Of course you must go, Rose. You're in charge of the job, aren't you?' Kerry had said, her voice sounding slightly puzzled. 'Go where you need to go; the prince is paying.'

Oh, yes, the prince was paying all right, and in paying the prince was also managing to demonstrate just how wide-reaching were his influence and power.

And power was, Rose had to concede with a guilty shiver, a very potent aphrodisiac indeed. She must remember that. Khalim would not be blind to that fact either, which meant that she would have to be very, very careful not to let it all go to her head. She thought back to how she had greeted his suggestion.

'Where will I be staying?' she demanded, not caring that Philip had sucked in a horrified breath at the tone she was using. 'In a hotel, I hope?'

Khalim stilled. She really could be most insolent! If she were not quite so beautiful, he really would not have tolerated such disrespect. 'Maraban has internationally acclaimed hotels,' he told her smoothly. 'But as my guest you will naturally stay in my father's...'

Rose looked up as she picked up on his hesitation—the last man she would have expected being stuck for words. 'Your father's what?'

'Palace,' he said reluctantly.

Rose widened her eyes. His father's palace, no less! Well, of *course* he would have a palace, wouldn't he? Royal families did not generally live in trailer parks! She looked at him with interest, her indignation dissolving by the second.

Had his reluctance to speak been motivated by the fact that palaces were what really drew the line in the sand? Palaces were what emphasised the unbreachable differences between Khalim and ordinary people like her. And, if that was the case, then didn't that mean that there was a thoughtful streak running through him? Despite her reservations, she smiled.

'And is it a beautiful palace?' she asked him softly.

An answering smile curved the edges of Khalim's hard mouth. Most people rushed onto another subject—seeing his home simply as some kind of status symbol, forgetting that palaces tended to be designed with beauty in mind. But then Rose, he suspected, had a very real sense of the beautiful.

'Very.' His reply was equally soft. 'Would you like me to describe it to you, or will you wait and see for yourself?'

Rose swallowed down temptation. The very last thing she needed was that deep, sexy voice painting lyrical pictures for her. A voice like that could suck you in and transport you away to a magical place and make you have foolish wishes which could never come true. And Rose needed her feet set very firmly on the ground.

'No, I think I'll wait and see for myself, thank you,' she said primly, tucking her still pristine papers back into her briefcase. Khalim had promised to fill her in about the oil refinery on the plane and she was glad to agree. At least it would give them something to talk about, other than the kind of irritating questions which kept popping to the forefront of her mind, such as, Khalim, why are your lips so beautiful? Or, Khalim, did anyone ever tell you that you have a body to die for?

'Rose!'

Rose blinked out of her reverie to find Lara staring at her as if she were an alien who had just landed from the planet Mars. 'Wh-what is it?' she stumbled.

'You looked miles away!'

'I was.' In Maraban and in Khalim's arms again, to be precise. Wondering if the land he had described could ever possibly live up to the richness of his description of it. I hope not, she thought distractedly. I really do.

'When are you going?' asked Lara.

'The day after tomorrow.' Khalim had wanted to fly out

first thing the next morning, but Rose had put her foot down. She might have a wardrobe which could cope with almost any eventuality, but a trip such as this required a dash round London's biggest department stores! And hadn't it been immensely pleasurable to see his incredulous expression when she had opposed his wishes to leave when *he* wanted? She'd heard Philip's disbelieving snort as she'd refused to back down!

Who knew? Khalim was a man used to always getting his own way, and thwarting his wishes occasionally might just be good for him! Why, he might even thank her for it one day!

'Very well,' he had agreed coldly. 'The day after tomorrow.'

She spent the next day shopping and on impulse bought a new evening gown far more glittering and ostentatious than any of her normal purchases. But once she'd packed she felt almost sick with nerves, and realised that she'd better tell her parents she was going abroad. She rang and rang their old farmhouse, but there was no reply, and so she phoned her brother instead.

'Jamie? It's me, Rose!'

'Well, hi! How much do you want to borrow?' came back the dry comment.

'Very funny!'

'But you never seem to ring me these days, sister dearest—'

'You've lost the use of your dialling finger, have you? Men are notoriously bad at communication and I don't see why it should always be the women who stay in touch!'

Jamie sounded indulgent. 'Fair! So is this just a friendly chat with your favourite brother?'

'My only brother.' Rose smiled, and then grimaced at her reflection in the mirror. 'Well, actually, no—I've been trying to ring Mum and Dad—but there's no reply.'

'That's because they're up in the Lake District—'

'They're *always* going somewhere!'

'But it's good, isn't it? That they're enjoying their retirement—I hope *I'm* still having such a good time, at their age!'

'Yes,' said Rose thoughtfully. 'I wanted to tell them that I'm going abroad for a couple of days.'

'Oh? Anywhere nice?'

Rose removed a speck of dust from the mirror with her fingernail. 'Have you heard of a place called Maraban?'

There was a pause. 'Isn't it in the Middle East?'

'That's right.'

'So is it work? Or a holiday?'

'Oh, work. I've, er, been asked to find someone to head up their oil refinery.'

She could hear the frown in Jamie's voice. 'Really? But I thought you only worked in advertising?'

'Usually I do.' She scowled in the mirror again as if Khalim's reflection was mocking back at her. 'But this is special, or rather the client is. He's a…um…he's a prince.'

'Sorry? Must be a bad line—I thought you said he was a prince.'

How far-fetched it sounded! Her voice sounded almost apologetic. 'I did. He's Prince Khalim of Maraban.'

There was a moment of astounded silence before she could hear Jamie expelling air from between pursed lips—an expression of bemusement he had had since he was a little boy. Then he said, 'Wow! Lucky girl!'

'Aren't I?' she agreed, just hoping that it sounded convincing, because most women *would* be thrilled and excited by the idea, wouldn't they? 'You can tell all your friends I'm going to stay in a palace!'

'Heck,' he said softly, still sounding slightly stunned.

'And the other thing—'

'Mmm?'

'It's just that Lara's going to be away filming, and I just wondered whether you would pop your head into the flat on your way home from work—just check that there aren't any free newspapers or letters making it look like the flat is empty?'

'Course I will,' he replied cheerfully. 'You should try living somewhere that doesn't have such a high quota of burglars!'

'I know.' Rose let out a small sigh. 'Listen, thanks, Jamie.'

'Sure.' There was another pause. 'Rose, this trip—it *is* all perfectly above board, isn't it?'

'Of course it is! What else would it be? It's business, Jamie, strictly business.'

But as she replaced the receiver, Rose wondered if she had been entirely honest with her brother...

The following morning, she opened the door and her mouth fell open when she discovered that it was Khalim himself who stood there.

He saw the pink pout of her lips and smiled a predatory smile. 'Surprised?' he murmured. 'Were you expecting Philip?'

Well, yes, she was surprised, but not because he hadn't sent his emissary to collect her. Mainly because he had switched roles again. Gone was the exotic-looking businessman in the beautifully cut suit. Instead, he was dressed in a variation of the outfit he'd been wearing at the wedding—a flowing, silken top with loose trousers of the same material worn underneath. But today the robes were more silvery than gold. A colder colour altogether, providing an austere backdrop to the dark, proud features. Oh, but he looked magnificent!

'You've ch-changed,' was all she could breathlessly manage.

'Of course I have. I'm going home,' came the simple reply. 'Are you ready?'

She'd packed just one suitcase, and it stood in readiness in the hall. She gestured to it and then *was* surprised when he picked it up.

He saw the look and correctly interpreted it. 'You imagined that I would send someone up to collect it? That I should
never carry anyone else's bags?'

'I suppose I did.'

Astonishingly, he found that he wanted to enlighten her—
to show her that he was not just a man who had been cosseted
by servants from the moment of his birth.

'There were reasons behind me being sent to boarding-
school other than to learn to blend into both societies,' he
told her softly. 'Like cold showers and rigorous sport and the
discipline of learning to stand on my own two feet.'

She stared at him, all too aware of the dark luminosity of
his eyes. 'And was it hard?' she questioned. 'To adapt to a
new culture and all that went with it?'

Her direct questions went straight to the very heart of the
matter; impossible to ignore or to brush aside. He shrugged.
'Little boys can be cruel.'

'Yes, I know.' She wondered if he was conscious that remembered pain had clouded the amazing black eyes. 'And
how did you cope with that?'

He pulled the door open and motioned for her to precede
him. 'You have to appear not to care. Only then will you
cease to become the butt of playground mockery.'

She saw a picture of a beautiful young boy with hair as
black as his eyes. Outstanding in more than just looks and
an easy target for boys who had not had so many of life's
gifts conferred on them.

'Khalim—'

She was close enough for him to feel the sweet warmth of
her breath. Close enough for him to have coiled his fingers
around the narrow indentation of her waist and to have pulled
her to him, and kissed her.

Would she have resisted? He doubted it. No woman who
had ever been kissed by him had failed to follow it up by
tumbling into bed with him. But the timing was wrong. Why
begin something only to have it end unsatisfactorily? If he

made love to her now, then it would be a swift coupling in her bedroom—with no guarantee that the flatmate would not suddenly return. And Philip and the chauffeur sitting waiting downstairs in the car. That would do her reputation no good at all, he realised—shocked that it should matter to him.

'Let's go,' he said, and moved away from her before his body picked up any more of her enticing signals.

The long black car soon picked up speed once they were out of the clutches of the city itself and heading towards Heathrow Airport.

Khalim, rather surprisingly, took out a laptop computer and sat tapping away at it for the entire journey, leaving Rose with little to do other than to pull out a book to read, which was at least a distraction from the unnerving presence of the man by her side.

She was reading *Maraban—Land of Dreams and Contrasts*, by Robert Cantle, a weighty book and, apparently, the definitive work on the country, which she'd bought on yesterday afternoon's shopping trip. She'd expected to have to wade through it, but she couldn't have been more wrong. It was, she thought to herself dreamily, absolutely *fascinating*.

Khalim glanced over at where she sat engrossed, and raised his dark brows.

'Not exactly what you'd call light reading,' he observed.

She heard the surprise in his voice. 'You expected me to sit flicking through magazines, I suppose?'

'Never suppose, Rose,' he returned softly. 'Never with me.'

In the confines of the luxurious car, his proximity overwhelmed her and she found herself edging a little further up the leather seat away from him. 'I'm enjoying it,' she told him solidly.

'You *do* take your work seriously, don't you?' he commented drily.

She looked up and treated him to a cool stare. 'Please don't patronise me, Khalim. The more I know about Maraban, the better I am able to do my job.'

He smiled, and settled back to his screen, thinking that Rose Thomas was proving to be much, much more than a pretty face. A *very* pretty face.

His eyes flickered to where one shapely thigh was outlined beneath an ankle-length skirt in a filmy, pale blue material which matched the simple cashmere sweater she wore. She'd dressed appropriately, he thought with pleasure.

He'd had many Western lovers, but none who seemed to have such a genuine interest in his country. Plenty who had *pretended* to, he remembered. His mouth hardened. But they had been the matrimonially ambitious ones, and as easy to spot as the glittering sapphire—as big as a swan's egg— which dominated the crown he would one day inherit.

He glanced out of the window, knowing that he would soon have to face the reality of his destiny. For that very morning had come news from Maraban that his father was frailer than before. Pain etched little lines on his brow as he acknowledged that the mantle of responsibility had slipped a little closer to his shoulders.

Would this be his last, delicious fling before it descended completely? he wondered.

Rose had never been on a private jet before and the interior of the Lear matched up to her wildest expectations. Most of the seats had been removed to provide a spacious interior, and two stewardesses were in attendance.

Very much in attendance, thought Rose grimly, suspecting that both had been chosen for their decorative qualities as much as for their undoubted efficiency. And both, like herself, were blonde—though these blondes had not had their colouring bestowed on them by nature.

Khalim introduced her to the pilot, who was obviously a fellow Marabanesh, and once they had effected a smooth take-off he turned to her, studying her mutinous expression with amusement.

'Does something displease you, Rose? Is something wrong?'

She certainly wasn't going to tell him that in her opinion the stewardesses could have done with wearing something which resembled a skirt, instead of a pelmet. She met his eyes, and once again her heart thundered in her ears. 'Wrong?' she managed, as smoothly as she could. 'What on earth could be wrong, Khalim?'

He had hoped that she was jealous; he wanted her to be jealous.

In fact, he had slept with neither of the attendants, even though it would have taken nothing more than a careless snap of the fingers to do so. He suspected that the two women would have been game for almost anything—and that even a *ménage à trois* would have been greeted with delight, instead of derision. But he would never have sullied himself with such a dalliance, even though he knew that many of his cousins enjoyed such debauchery.

'Shall we eat something?' he questioned as the taller of the stewardesses approached them.

She remembered what he had said to her in the restaurant. She'd never felt less like eating in her life, but to refuse would surely be an insult to his chef? 'Yes, please.'

'And we will drink mint tea,' he instructed.

'Sir.' The stewardess inclined her blonde head respectfully.

The two attendants began laying out a feast on the low, circular table. Rose looked down at the engraved bronze plates, enjoying the colour and variety of the different foods which they held—tiny portions which pleased the eye and tempted the palate.

'You like these things?' asked Khalim as he offered her a tiny pancake stuffed with cheese and doused with syrup, resisting the urge to feed her, morsel by morsel, then have her lick his fingers clean.

'I've never tried food like this before.' She bit into it. 'Mmm! It's yummy!'

'Yummy?' He smiled as he observed her, enjoying the unconscious sensuality of watching her eat. 'Then you have many pleasures in store, Rose,' he told her, his voice deepening as he thought of the ultimate pleasure she would enjoy with him.

Something in his voice drove all thoughts of food clean out of her mind, and she lifted her head to find herself imprisoned in the black gleam of his eyes. She put the half-eaten pancake down with fingers which were threatening to shake.

He hadn't touched a thing himself, she thought, as he chose just that moment to languidly stretch his long legs out, and the brush of the silk as it defined the muscular thrust of his thighs was positively *indecent*.

'Something is troubling you, Rose?' he murmured.

'Nothing,' she lied and directed her gaze to his chest instead, but that wasn't much better. She found herself imagining what his torso would be like without its silken covering—hard and dark, she guessed, with the skin lightly gleaming like oiled satin. 'N-nothing at all.'

He saw the swift rise of colour to her cheeks and the sudden darkening of her eyes. He could order everyone to clear the main salon now, he thought heatedly. And take her quickly before this hunger became much more intense.

But what if she cried aloud with pleasure? Sobbed her fulfilment in his arms as women inevitably did? Did he really want the two attendants exchanging glances as they listened at the door while he made hard, passionate love to her?

'Eat some more,' he urged huskily.

'I...I'm full.'

He glanced at his watch. 'Then I shall order for these plates to be removed—'

'And then you'll tell me all about Maraban's oil refinery?'

she put in quickly, because at least that would take her mind off things. Him.

The oil refinery? He threw her a look of mocking bemusement as he leaned back against the cushions. Never had a woman surprised him quite so much as Rose Thomas and surprise was rare enough to be a novelty! 'That is what you would like?' he questioned gravely.

'More than anything in the world!' she agreed fervently, but the gleam of discernment in the black eyes told her that they both knew she was lying.

He spoke knowledgeably for almost an hour, while Rose butted in with intelligent questions. The first time she asked him something, he raised his eyebrows in a look which would have made most people freeze and then retreat.

'I need to *ask* you these things,' explained Rose patiently, reminding herself that maybe it wasn't *his* fault that people usually hung on adoringly to every word he said.

'Such pertinent questions,' he conceded in a murmur.

'There you go again, patronising me!' she chided.

'That was not my intention, I can assure you.'

She paused, unsure whether to frame the question she *really* wanted to ask, and then remonstrating with herself for an uncharacteristic lack of courage. 'Khalim?'

His eyes narrowed, some instinct telling him that this was not another query about Maraban's oil output. 'Rose?' he returned softly.

'Just why *did* you want me to act as your head-hunter?'

He curved her a slow, almost cruel smile. 'I had to have you.'

Rose froze. 'You mean—'

He shook his head. 'I was informed that you were the best head-hunter in town—I already told you that.'

'Thank you.'

Her blue eyes shone a challenge at him and he found himself smiling in response. 'You also asked me whether I had employed you so that I could seduce you.'

Some of her customary grit returned and she didn't flinch beneath his mocking gaze. 'But you neatly avoided answering me, didn't you, Khalim?'

'Did I?'

'You know you did.'

He narrowed her a speculative glance, then shrugged. 'I can't deny that I find you beautiful, or that I want you in my bed, but—'

She sucked in a breath which was both shocked and yet profoundly excited. The men she knew just didn't *say* things like that! 'But what?'

'Sleeping with me isn't a prerequisite for landing the contract.'

'But will I get a bonus if I *do* succumb to your charms?' she asked flippantly.

Khalim's face darkened and he very nearly pulled her to him to punish her with a kiss which would dare her to ever mock him so again. But he stopped himself in time; instead, he forced himself to imagine how sweet the victory would be after such a protracted battle!

'Put it this way,' he warned her silkily, 'that as a man I will attempt to seduce you—no red-blooded Marabanesh would do otherwise.' A slow, glittering look. 'But you are perfectly within your rights to turn me down.'

Rose stared at him as she felt the irrevocable unfurling of desire, knowing that his words were iced with an implicit boast. That no woman Khalim attempted to lure to bed would ever be able to resist him.

And Rose had spent her life resisting men who saw her as just a trophy girlfriend, with her blonde hair and her bright blue eyes. Just you wait and see, Prince Khalim! she thought.

He was intrigued by the defiant little tilt of her chin, and his need for her grew. He controlled his desire with an effort and distracted himself by flicking another glance at his watch.

'Do you want to look out of the window?' he asked unsteadily. 'We're coming into Maraban.'

CHAPTER SIX

SUNLIGHT danced and shimmered across a wide expanse of water, and Rose was spellbound—enough to be impervious to the sudden build-up of tension which his silken words had produced.

'Water!' she exclaimed as the beauty of the scene below momentarily drove all her newly learned facts about the country straight out of her head. 'But I thought—'

'That you would be coming to a barren and desolate land with not a drop of water in sight?' he chided. 'That is the Caspian Sea, Rose, and the borders of Maraban lie on its Western shores.'

'Oh, but it's beautiful!'

'You seem to think everything *about* Maraban is beautiful,' he commented indulgently.

'But it is!'

He thought how wonderfully uninhibited her appreciation was, and how her eyes sparkled like the blue waters of the Caspian itself.

'Fasten your seat belt,' he murmured gently. 'The heat can sometimes make the landing turbulent.

But, in the event, their descent to Maraban was as smooth as honey, and as the plane taxied down the runway Rose could see a large number of men standing in line, all in flowing robes which fluttered in the small breeze created by the aircraft.

'Gosh, it's a deputation,' she observed.

Khalim leaned across her and glanced out of the window, and her senses were invaded by the subtle persuasion of sandalwood.

'I shall go out alone,' he told her. 'If you want to go and freshen up.'

'So you don't want to risk being seen with me, Khalim?' she asked wryly. 'Are you planning to smuggle me off the plane with a blanket over my head?

He wondered if she had any idea how privileged she was to accompany him in this way! If it had been anyone else, he would have flown them over separately. But he had not wanted to take the risk of her refusing to come...

'I don't imagine that you would wish to be subjected to the wild conjecture which your appearance would inevitably provoke.' His tone was dry. 'The less we announce your presence, the less tongues in the city will gossip.'

She got some idea then of how public his life had to be, and how rare the opportunity to play any of it out in private, and, in spite of everything, she felt her heart soften.

'Yes, of course. I understand.' She nodded. 'I'll go and freshen up as you suggested.'

He laughed. 'Why, Rose—that's the most docile I've ever heard you be!'

She put on a suitably meek expression. 'And you like my docility do you, Oh, Prince?'

The breath caught in his throat and dried it to sawdust and his heart clenched inside his chest. 'No. I like you fiery,' he told her honestly. 'You make a worthy combatant.'

Which pleased her far more than remarks about the colour of her hair or the sapphire glitter of her eyes. Her looks she'd been born with and were just the luck of the draw—her personality was a different matter. And if Khalim approved of certain facets of her nature...now, that really *was* a compliment!

Just don't get carried away by compliments, she reminded herself.

She enjoyed the luxury of the aircraft's bathroom, which contained the most heavenly sandalwood soap. Rose picked it up and sniffed it, her eyes closing for a moment. It smelt of *him*. She washed her hands and her face with it, and it was as though the essence of Khalim had seeped into her skin itself.

Stop it, she told herself as she brushed her hair and slicked on a little lipstick. You're walking straight into his honeytrap.

She stepped back to survey the results in the mirror, thinking that at least she *looked* cool and unflappable. Only the slightly hectic glitter of her eyes betrayed the fact that inside she was churned up by conflicting emotions—and the most disturbing one of all was the fact that Khalim was beginning to grow on her.

Grow on her? Who did she think she was kidding? Why, it was as if he had taken up root inside her mind and managed to invade most of her waking thoughts. Whatever had she thought about before Khalim had entered her life?

After twenty minutes, he returned to the aircraft, by which time Philip had joined her in the main salon.

'Rose and I will go in the second car with the bodyguard,' said Khalim imperturbably. 'Will you take the first car and prepare them at the palace for my arrival?'

'Of course.' Philip gave Rose a curious glance, before bowing to the prince.

'Why does he look at me that way?' asked Rose, after he had gone.

For a second he experienced a rare moment of indulgence. 'What way is that, sweet Rose?'

'You saw.'

Khalim sighed. Would the truth go to her head? Fool her into believing that her presence here had an ultra-special significance? Or a future?

'Because you are the first woman I have ever brought here to Maraban,' he admitted, on a growl.

She didn't react. 'Should I be flattered by that?' she questioned drily.

He found her coolness utterly irresistible. Even though it *was* rather galling to be shown nothing in the way of gratitude! 'I would not dare to presume it—not of you,' he murmured. 'Come, Rose—enough of this sparring—let me show you my country.'

The hot air hit her with a heated jolt, even though it was now September and Khalim informed her that the temperatures were already cooling down towards the icy winter which followed.

And the drive to the palace was a feast to the senses! Rose stared out of the limousine window with fascination at the scenes which unfolded before her. Maraban's capital was absolutely heaving with people and there were cars and carts and camels all vying for space along the congested roads of the city. She could see dusty boxes of oranges, and live chickens in a cage.

The main thoroughfare had obviously been cleared for Khalim's arrival, and she could see crowds jostling to catch a glimpse of the enigmatic profile through the smoked-glass window.

The palace was some way out from the main drag of the city, and Rose's first sight of it was unforgettable. In the distance, tall mountains reared up in jagged peaks, and against the cloudless blue cobalt of the sky stood the palace itself—gleaming purest gold in the honeyed light of the afternoon sun.

Rose was silent and Khalim looked at her, taken aback by the rapture which had softened her features into dreamy wonder.

'You like my home?' he asked, knowing deep down that such a question was redundant.

It seemed unbelievable that such an extraordinary building could ever be described by the comfortable word 'home'.

'How could I not like it?' she questioned simply.

Khalim's mouth hardened. Was she really as guileless as she seemed? Or was she cynically aware that her eyes were like dazzling blue saucers when she spoke with such emotion, their light lancing straight to his very heart?

He shook his head slightly in negation. He wanted her body, that was all.

That was all.

'Tell me what to expect when we arrive,' said Rose, wondering why he was scowling when all she had done was tell him she liked his home.

Sometimes, he reflected ruefully, she sounded as if *she* were the one expressing a royal command! 'My mother and sisters have their own section of the palace—we will join them for dinner and you will meet them then. You will have your own suite of rooms, and a girl will be assigned to look after your needs.'

'And your father?'

'My father lives in a different section of the building.'

She hesitated. 'Because he's sick, you mean?'

Khalim frowned. 'You are very persistent, Rose! No, not simply because he is sick—it is our royal custom. Princes of Maraban do not sleep with their women, not even their wives.'

Rose looked at him in disbelief. 'You mean that they just go and have *sex* with them, and then go back to their own apartments?'

'*Sometimes* they remain there for the night,' he informed her benignly, though he could not imagine leaving *her* alone for one precious second of the night.

'Lucky old them!' said Rose sarcastically.

'Actually,' he iced back, 'they *would* show gratitude, yes!'

'For being downtrodden, you mean?'

'I think you forget yourself, Rose!' he snapped.

'I think not! I am not your royal subject, Khalim! And if I have an opinion which happens to differ from yours—well, that's just *tough*!'

He had never felt so turned on by a woman in his life and the desire to kiss her was overwhelming. But by then the car was driving slowly into the inner courtyard where trees provided a welcome shade—the sunlight dappling through broad, verdant leaves. Khalim clicked his tongue with irritation as the chauffeur opened the door for her.

But when Rose alighted from the car, she was hit with the most unforgettable and heady fragrance, so powerful that it halted her in her tracks.

'What is that amazing scent?' she whispered, their disagreement forgotten.

A sense of destiny whispered disturbing fingers over his flesh. 'It is the fragrance of the roses which bloom in the palace gardens,' he murmured, watching as the sun turned her hair into a gold just a shade lighter than the palace itself. 'The sweetest scent in the world—but you must wait until the evening time, when the perfume is increased by a hundredfold.'

But as they walked side by side towards a pair of vast, ornate doors, he thought that no scent could be sweeter than the subtle perfume which drifted from her skin, more beguiling than any siren.

Robed figures awaited them, and Rose was introduced, certain that she would never be able to remember all these new and unusual names. The men all bowed courteously but she could detect flashes of curiosity on their hard, dark faces. I wonder if they approve of me, she thought, but then found Khalim's gaze on her face, more encouraging than she could have believed it would be, and she felt the warmth of his protection.

And all the while she felt that they were surrounded by other watchers, by unseen eyes. She caught a brief glimpse of a young woman, spectacularly clad in crimson silk, but when she turned her head to get a better look the woman had disappeared again.

Khalim followed the direction of her gaze. 'Fatima!' he called, and the young woman reappeared, only her eyes visible above a scarlet yashmak.

She performed an elaborate sort of bow, and Khalim said,

'This is Rose Thomas. I have brought her here to do a job for me. I want you to make sure that she has everything she needs. Say hello now, Fatima.'

'Good afternoon,' said Fatima, in a soft, halting English accent. 'I am pleased to meet you.'

Khalim laughed. 'Fatima is learning English!'

'I'm impressed,' said Rose gravely. 'And rather ashamed that my Marabanese only amounts to about five words.'

Khalim glimmered her an onyx gaze. 'I will teach you,' he promised softly. Oh, yes. He would teach her the many words of love. She would learn to please him in his own language. 'Now Fatima will show you to your rooms—and you shall bathe and change—then later I will come for you.'

She wanted to ask him exactly what he meant by such a masterful and yet ambiguous expression as that—*I will come for you*—but it didn't really seem appropriate, not with Fatima hanging onto every word. He probably meant that he would come to take her down for dinner. So why did that make her heart crash against her ribcage in disappointment?

'Come, please,' said Fatima, with a shy smile.

Rose followed her through a maze of silent marble corridors, thinking that unless she had a guide she would get hopelessly lost.

At last Fatima opened a set of double-doors leading into a large, cool room and Rose looked around her, her eyes feasting themselves on the richly embroidered cushions which were scattered over a wide, low bed covered in a throw of embroidered gold. A carved wooden chest stood in one corner, and the room smelt faintly of incense—though a bronze vase which was crammed full of crimson roses only added to the perfumed atmosphere.

One wall contained bookshelves and closer inspection showed a variety of novels and textbooks, some in Marabanese, but mostly in English. Well, at least she would not be bored!

The shutters were closed but Fatima went over to the window and opened them, and outside Rose could see a profusion of blooms of every hue and their scent drifted in to bewitch her.

The rose garden!

Had Khalim deliberately put her in here, to enchant her with their fragrance? To remind her of the flower she had been named after?

She shivered as a sense of the irrevocable washed cool temptation over her skin.

'You will bathe?' asked Fatima, and gestured towards a door leading off the enormous room.

'Yes, yes, please—I will.'

'And you wish me to assist you?'

Rose shook her head, and smiled, thinking how different Maraban hospitality was! 'No, thanks, Fatima—I'm used to managing on my own,' she answered gravely.

Fatima nodded and gave another shy smile. 'I will bring mint tea in an hour.'

'That will be wonderful. Thank you.'

After the girl had left, Rose went into the bathroom to find a deep circular bath, inlaid with exquisite mosaics in every conceivable shade of blue. There were fragrances and essences from Paris, and fluffy towels as big as sheets. East meets West, she thought with approval, and turned the taps on.

It was the best bath she had ever had. Lying submerged in scented bubbles in the high, cool splendour of the vaulted bathroom, she felt that the real Rose Thomas was a very long way away indeed. So why did she suddenly feel more *alive* than she had ever felt before?

By the time she had dried her hair, it was getting on for seven o'clock. When would Khalim come, and what should she wear for dinner? Would her gorgeous new evening gown make her look like some kind of houri?

In the end, she decided on a simple silk dress which brushed the floor when she walked. The sleeves were long and loose and it was the soft, intense colour of bluebells. Her hair she left loose and shining, and as she stared at herself in the long mirror she thought that she could not possibly offend anyone's sensibilities in such a modest gown.

Fatima came, bearing a bronze tray of mint tea. In true Eastern style, Rose settled herself on an embroidered cushion on the floor, and had just poured herself a cup when there was an authoritative rap on the door. Her heart began to thunder.

'Come in,' she called.

The door opened and there stood Khalim. He, too, had changed, and he must also have bathed, for his black hair was still damp and glittered with a halo of stray drops of water. His robes were coloured deepest claret—like rich, old wine—but his face looked hard, his expression forbidding as he quietly shut the door behind him.

'Do you always invite men so freely into your bedroom, Rose?' he questioned softly.

She put the cup down and looked up at him, knowing that she was not prepared to tolerate his insulting implication. Nor prepared to admit that she had known it was him, simply from the assertive way he had knocked on the door! She shrugged her shoulders in a devil-may-care gesture. 'Oh, they usually come in two at a time! At least!'

'Please do not be flippant with me, Rose!' he exploded.

'Well, what do you expect?' she demanded. 'I *presumed* that no one would come here, except for you! And I *presumed* that while I was here I would be under your protection, but maybe I was wrong!'

'No.' His voice was heavy. He was used to obedience, not passionate logic from his women. 'No, you were not wrong.'

'Well, then—don't imply that I am loose with my favours—'

'Rose—'

'And don't you *dare* make a value judgement about me, when you barely know me, Khalim!'

Barely *know* her? Why, his conversations with Rose Thomas had been more intimate than those he'd had with any other woman before! He felt he knew her *very* well, and he had certainly told her more about himself than was probably wise. His voice gentled as he slid onto a cushion opposite her. 'Do you want me to know you better, Rose?'

Shockingly, she did—she wanted him to know her as intimately as any man could. She wanted to see the contrast of his long-limbed dark body entwined with the milky curves of her own. She wanted to feel the primitive thrust of his passion, the honeyed wonder of his kiss. She stared down at the clear chartreuse colour of her mint tea, afraid that he would see the hunger in her eyes.

'Rose?'

His voice was beguiling, but she resisted it. 'What?'

'Look at me.'

Compelled to obey by the command in his voice, she slowly lifted her head to find herself dazzled by a gaze of deepest ebony.

The pink flush which had gilded her pale skin pleased him, as did the darkened widening of those beautiful blue eyes. 'Do you want me to know you better?' he repeated on a sultry whisper.

The question was laced with erotic expectation, and a passive side she never knew existed wanted to gasp out, Oh, yes. Yes, *please!* But such capitulation must be par for the course for a man like Khalim. She would never win his respect if she fell like a ripe plum into those tempting arms. And his respect, she realised with a start, was what she wanted more than anything.

His body he would give her freely; his deference would be a far more elusive prize.

'Obviously—' she forced a breezy smile '—we will get to know each other better during my stay here. I have no objection to that, Khalim.'

It was such a deliberate misunderstanding that, instead of

feeling indignant, he began to laugh softly. 'You wilfully misunderstand me, Rose,' he murmured. 'You are quite outrageous.'

How rare the sound of his laughter, thought Rose with a sudden pang of compassion. How often could a man like this really let himself go?

She smiled and lifted up one of the china cups. 'Tea, Khalim?' she enquired.

He was still laughing when they went down to dinner.

As he guided her through the maze of marble corridors towards the dining hall, Rose wondered how he had spent his afternoon. Would it seem prying if she asked? 'Have you seen your father yet?' she asked softly.

His face tightened with pain and if she could have wished the words unsaid, she would have done so.

'I'm sorry, I didn't mean to—'

'No.' He shook his dark head. 'We cannot ignore reality, however painful it is. Yes, I saw him.' He paused. He could not talk freely to his mother or his sisters about his father's failing health, for they would begin to weep inconsolably. Nor Philip either. Philip was a man, and men discussed feelings only with discomfort. But Khalim had a sudden need to express himself—to articulate his fears. This was death which he was soon to encounter and he had known no close deaths other than his grandparents' when he had been away at school in England.

'He is fading.' He forced himself to say the brutal words, as if saying them would give life to them. Or death to them, he thought bleakly.

'I'm so sorry.' For one brief moment he looked so vulnerable that she longed to take him in her arms and lay his proud, beautiful face down on her shoulder and to hug him and comfort him. But surely such a gesture would be misinterpreted—even if it *was* her place to offer him solace, which it certainly wasn't.

But then the moment was gone anyway, for the face had resumed its proud and haughty demeanour as he inclined his head in wordless thanks for her commiseration.

'Let us go and eat,' he said.

Dinner was a curious affair, made even more so by the fact that Rose felt as though she was on show—which she guessed she was. But even more curious was Khalim's mother's initial reaction to her.

Khalim ushered Rose into the room where a very elegant woman aged about sixty sat with her two daughters at the long, rectangular table.

The three women wore lavishly embroidered robes, and Rose noticed that Khalim's mother's sloe-shaped black eyes narrowed and her shoulders stiffened with a kind of disbelief as Rose walked rather nervously into the ornate salon. She said something very quickly to her son in Marabanese, and Khalim nodded, his eyes narrowing thoughtfully.

But once Khalim had introduced them, she relaxed with a graciousness which disarmed her and shook Rose's hand and bid her welcome.

'What should I call you?' asked Rose nervously.

'You should call me Princess Arksoltan.' His mother gave her a surprisingly warm smile. 'My son must respect your work very much if he has accompanied you to Maraban.'

Khalim scanned his mother's face, but it bore no trace of disapproval. And why should it? She knew him well, and, yes, he *did* respect Rose's professional skills. His mother also read voraciously and that had, in its way, made her outlook unusually unfettered by tradition.

Perhaps she suspected that he would consummate his relationship with Rose while she was here. But that would not worry her either—she was as aware as he was that he must marry a woman of Maraban blood. She would turn a blind eye to any dalliances which occurred before that marriage would take place. As soon it must, he reminded himself, re-

membering the prospective brides who had been paraded before him just before he had flown out for Guy's wedding.

A host of dark-eyed virgins, their faces concealed by their
yashmaks. Young and exquisitely beautiful, not one had
dared meet his eye. He had asked himself whether he found
any of them attractive, and the answer had been yes, of
course he did. A man would have to have been made of stone
not to. But their inexperience and respect for his position
would make them merely hostages to his desires. By definition, it would be a submissive and unequal marriage.

He looked at Rose, at the proud way she bore herself and
the confidence with which she returned his stare. He felt the
muffled acceleration of his heart and cursed it.

'And these are my two sisters,' he said huskily. 'Caiusine
and Enegul.'

His two sisters were impossibly beautiful with black eyes
and the thickest falls of ebony hair imaginable. And none of
the women wore yashmaks, Rose noted in surprise as she
took her place at the table, with Khalim on one side, his
mother on the other.

Soundless servants brought platter upon platter of food,
while candles guttered on the table, blown by the scented
breeze which drifted in through the open windows.

'Will you drink wine, Rose?' Khalim asked her softly,
watching the rise and fall of her breathing and the way it
elevated her magnificent breasts.

She shook her head. 'I won't, thank you. I'll have what
everyone else is having.'

Khalim poured her juice, silently applauding her for her
diplomacy, while Rose chatted about the purpose of her trip
in answer to his sisters' interested questions.

'Tomorrow we're going to the oil refinery,' she told them.

'And Khalim is letting *you* choose Murad's successor?'
asked Enegul in astonishment.

Black eyes glittered at her through the candlelight and his

sister's question only crystallised what Rose had suspected all along.

'I think that Khalim has already decided who he wants to replace Murad,' said Rose slowly as the absurdity of the situation dawned on her. As if a man of Khalim's power would rely solely on *her* judgement! 'And I'm just here to confirm his decision.'

He felt the dry beat of desire. Obviously, she was nothing but a witch—well schooled in the art of sorcery! 'How very perceptive of you, Rose.'

'That's my job,' she answered sweetly.

'And what if you and Khalim disagree?' asked Arksoltan. Black clashed with blue in visual duel.

'Then it's whoever argues the case for their choice best, I guess,' said Rose.

'Khalim, then!' put in the younger sister loyally.

'Do not underestimate the power of Rose's debating skills,' came his dry response.

He accompanied her back to her room, and the corridors were echoing and silent, empty save for the ever-constant presence of his bodyguard who followed at a discreet distance behind them.

Her senses were full of him as they walked side by side. The whisper of the silk as it clung and fluttered around the hard, lean body and the faint drift of sandalwood from the warmth of his skin. But there was an unmistakable tension about him, and it had transmitted itself to her so that her breathing had become unsteady, her heart rate erratic as she thought of what *could* lie ahead.

Would he try to kiss her tonight? And didn't she, if she was being honest—and she spent her life trying to be honest—didn't she want that more than anything else?

'You have enjoyed your evening with my family, Rose?'

She nodded. 'I thought it very good of your mother to entertain me when she must be so worried about your father.'

'To be royal means to learn to hide your feelings.' He

shrugged. 'And it would be unforgivable not to show hospitality.'

She nodded, and thought of his mother's initial reaction to her. 'When I walked into the dining room, your mother looked...'

He stilled. 'What?'

'I don't know—shocked—surprised.' She shrugged. 'Something, anyway.'

'Is there anything which escapes those perceptive eyes of yours?' he demanded.

'And she said something to you, too—something in Marabanese which I couldn't understand.'

He nodded.

'What was it, Khalim?'

He gave a painful sigh, knowing that he could not be evasive with her, could not resist the sapphire appeal in her eyes. Was this destiny he was about to recount, or simply history? Coincidence, even? 'You bear a strong resemblance to a woman my great-great-grandfather knew.'

She stared at him, wondering what he wasn't telling her.

He seemed to make his mind up about something. 'Come with me,' he said, and changed the direction in which they were walking.

Intrigued, Rose quickened her step to match his. 'Where are you taking me?' she whispered.

'You will see.'

The chamber he took her to was so carefully hidden that no one could have found it, certainly not unless they were intended to. A small, almost secret chamber containing nothing other than books and a desk, with a carved wooden stool.

And a portrait.

'Look,' said Khalim, very softly, and pointed to the painting. 'Look, Rose. Do you see the resemblance now?'

The air left her lungs of its own accord, and Rose sucked in a shuddering gasp of astonishment.

A portrait of a woman, whose flaxen hair was contrasted

against a gown of crimson silk, her blue eyes capturing the viewer—mesmerising, bright blue eyes which seemed to see into your very soul. Her face was pale, almost as pale as Rose's own skin and she knew without a doubt that this was no Marabanesh woman.

'Wh-who *is* it?' she whispered, and she only just prevented herself from saying, Is it *me*?

'A woman that Malik loved,' he told her tonelessly.

'And lost?' she guessed.

He shook his head sadly. 'She was never his to be had, Rose,' he said. 'The cultural differences between them were too great. And they discovered that love, in this particular case, could not conquer all. She returned to America and they never saw one another again.'

'Oh, but that's terrible!' she breathed.

'You think so? It was the only solution open to them, my sweet, romantic Rose.'

She discerned in his voice the emphatic acceptance of his own destiny, and she didn't say another word as he ushered her out of the room and back towards her own apartments.

'We are here.' He stopped outside her door and stared down at her for one long moment. 'And now...' he was aware of the sudden rapidity of his breathing, the erratic thundering of his heart '...you must sleep, or...'

'Or what?' she asked breathlessly.

He didn't answer at first, just raised his dark hand to lift a strand of the blonde hair which rippled down over her shoulders. 'So pale. Pale as the moon itself,' he whispered.

She stared up at him, too excited to be able to say a single word, other than his name. 'Khalim?' And it came out like a prayer.

He looked down into her eyes, read the unmistakable invitation in them and felt a heady rush of triumph wash over him, knowing that she wanted him, that he could pin her up against the wall and make her his.

He felt himself grow exquisitely hard in anticipation, until he drew himself up short and reminded himself that this was no ordinary woman. She was more beautiful than most, for a start. And a woman like this would surely spend her life warding off advances from men. Not that she would ever reject *him*, of course—but how many times would she have been made to wait for something she wanted? To simmer with desire? Until the slow heat of need became unbearable and boiled over into a heated fire?

And hadn't he become curiously *intimate* with this Rose? Confided in her in a way which was unknown to him? He had heard men say that sex combined with intimacy was the most mind-blowing experience of all. Could he not taste that pleasure once, just once, before his inevitable marriage?

He curved his mouth into a slow, almost cruel smile as he bent his head and briefly touched his lips to hers, feeling her instinctive shudder of elation being quickly replaced by one of disappointment as he swiftly lifted his head away from hers.

'Goodnight, sweet Rose,' he said softly, resisting the soft, blue temptation of her eyes. And he turned back along the wide, marbled corridor, the shadowy figure of his bodyguard immediately echoing his movements, and she watched him go with a sense of disbelief.

Had she been mistaken, then? Imagining that Khalim's not-so-hidden agenda had been to seduce her? And she had actually *accused* him of that? Oh, Lord! She leaned her forehead against the cool of the wall, recognising that she had just succeeded in making a complete and utter fool of herself.

CHAPTER SEVEN

BUT by the time she was dressed the following morning, Rose had recovered most of her equilibrium. The morning sun always had a habit of putting things into perspective. Okay, so Khalim hadn't made a pass at her—why, she should be celebrating, not moping around the place! Falling into his arms—which she had been all too ready and willing to do last night—was a sure-fire recipe for a broken heart. Her head had already told her that in no uncertain terms.

His authoritative rap sounded just after nine, but she went through the pantomime of asking, 'Who is it?' and hearing the reluctant trace of amusement in his voice as he replied. 'Khalim.'

She opened the door to find the ebony eyes mocking her. 'Good morning, Khalim,' she said innocently.

'I see you learn your lessons well,' he told her softly as he scanned her face for the tell-tale signs of crying. But there were none, and he was taken aback by a sense of disappointment that she had not wept in the night for his embrace.

And Rose knew exactly what he was thinking! Had he hoped to find her despondent? she wondered wryly. 'That depends on whether or not I have a good teacher!' she murmured.

'And am I?' he purred. 'A good teacher?'

She walked past him, knowing how dangerous this kind of conversation could be if she allowed it to continue. The seductive tilt to his question made her want to melt into his arms, and that was *not* on his agenda—he had made that *quite* clear. 'It doesn't require a lot of skill to tell someone not to open the door without first finding out who's there!'

Khalim's mouth hardened. Such impudence! So—today

she was refusing to play the game, was she? He wondered anew why had he not tasted the pleasures she had been all too willing to offer him last night, tasted them over and over again until he had grown bored with them?

'Let us go and eat breakfast!' he growled.

'Lovely,' she murmured.

They broke bread and ate fruit on a terrace which overlooked the tiered rose-gardens and the scent and sight of the flowers were almost too distracting. Just as Khalim was. And where had her appetite gone? Rose picked undisinterestedly at a pomegranate and drank juice instead.

'You aren't hungry?' he demanded irritatedly, because of his restless night racked with frustrated dreams.

'It's too hot.'

Too *something*, he thought, shifting slightly in his chair as if mere movement could dispel the rapidly building ache of longing deep inside him. 'We shall drink some coffee, and then leave.' He glanced down her long legs which were modestly covered in sage-green linen, matching the short-sleeved safari shirt which gave no emphasis to the curve of her bosom beneath. 'I see you have worn trousers.'

'I knew you would not want me showing any flesh.'

He bit back his instinctive comment that she could show him as much flesh as she wanted, and whenever she wanted.

'And I didn't know if I would have to climb stairs at the refinery,' she continued animatedly. 'So I played safe.'

'Yes.' His pulse hammered as he imagined her walking upstairs, worrying about her modesty. Affording him the occasional tantalising view of lace panties. A pulse began to hammer at his temple. She *would* wear lace, he was certain of that. And once they were lovers he would buy her a tiny little skirt and she would wear no panties at all, and he would demand that she climb the stairs in front of him...

'Khalim? Is something wrong?'

Her face was an enchanting picture of genuine concern, and Khalim glared. 'Nothing is wrong!' he snapped as his erotic daydream didn't *quite* do the decent thing of leaving him alone. 'But the sooner we get out to the refinery, the better!'

They drank their coffee in uncomfortable silence and then walked around to the front of the palace, where two gleaming four-wheel drives sat awaiting them.

Khalim went to the first and opened the passenger door for her and Rose looked over her shoulder to see that the second vehicle had a burly and shadowy figure at the driving seat.

'Who's in the other car?' she asked as he climbed in and turned the key in the ignition and the second vehicle started its engine in synchrony.

'My bodyguard,' he said shortly.

The ubiquitous bodyguard! 'Doesn't your bodyguard have a name?'

He gave a thin smile. 'I am monitored twenty-four hours a day, three hundred and sixty-five days a year, Rose,' he said. 'There are a team of them—faceless, nameless and invisible to all intents and purposes. It is better that way—if I build a relationship with any of them then it makes me...' He had been about to say vulnerable, but changed his mind. Khalim *vulnerable*? Never! 'Familiarity makes them more accessible to bribery,' he compromised.

She tried to imagine being watched all the time. 'And don't you ever feel trapped?'

'Trapped?' He considered the question as he turned right onto a wide, dusty road surrounded by sand which was the pale silvery colour of salt. 'I have never known any different,' he explained slowly. 'Even at school, I had someone there, a figure always in the background.'

'But don't you ever want to break free?' she asked wistfully.

Her voice held a trace of disquiet, and something in the way her face had softened made Khalim feel a sudden overwhelming sense of regret for what could never be. 'This is freedom of a kind,' he said simply. 'To be alone in a car with a beautiful woman, here in Maraban.'

She thought about this as the car effortlessly negotiated the pock-marked road. 'Why have you never brought a woman here before? There must have been...' She tried to be sophisticated but, stupidly, her voice threatened to crack. 'Lovers.'

There had been women, yes—many lovers in his thirty-five years. So why was it that he could not picture a single one of their faces? Nor recall one conversation which had enthralled him enough to stay locked in his memory?

'My family and my people would disapprove if I flaunted Western permissiveness in their faces.'

Rose flinched at his choice of phrase, but his attention was on the dusty horizon ahead of them, and he did not notice. Did he classify *her* as a permissive Westerner, then?

He tried to give her a brief picture of his existence. 'I live two types of life, Rose. The man who jets around the world and wears suits and stays in all the major cities—he is not the same man who dwells here in Maraban.'

'A man of contrasts,' she said slowly. 'From a land of contrasts.'

He was unable to resist a slow smile of delight. 'A few hours in my country and already you are an expert!'

That smile tore at her heart. Wasn't he aware of its devastating impact? Didn't he know he could ask for the moon with a smile like that—and very probably be given it on a shining golden platter? It just wasn't fair, thought Rose as she stared sightlessly out at the unforgiving desert. 'That's another part of my job,' she said. 'I learn very quickly.'

He wondered what had made her renew that flippant tone, or to sit so rigidly in her seat, but at that moment he saw the gleam of reflected light which heralded the first view of the refinery.

'Look, Rose,' he urged softly.

She forced herself to look interested, forcing herself to put thoughts of Khalim out of her mind. He wasn't hers. He never *could* be hers. What would Kerry say if she knew that her finest head hunter was sitting staring dismally ahead like a lovesick schoolgirl?

But the smile she had pinned onto her face became genuine as she stared at the maze of silver towers and pipes which appeared on the stark horizon.

'It's so modern!' she exclaimed. 'Like a space-age city!'

'You imagined camels, did you?' he questioned drily. 'Robed figures rolling barrels of crude oil around?'

'Maybe a bit,' she admitted.

'Maraban's refinery is one of the world's finest,' he told her, with a quiet pride. 'It takes billions to build a refinery and millions to maintain. Cost-cutting inevitably leads to breakdowns in the system, and we must be one hundred per cent reliable if we are to stay ahead of our competitors.'

There was a tough, uncompromising note to his voice, and in that moment she realised that he was far more than just a figurehead. He was *involved*. Caring. Passionate. About his country and its industry, if nothing else.

The guards at the heavily barred security gates, who had obviously been alerted to their arrival, bowed and ushered them through and Khalim drew up outside the simple but beautifully designed main entrance. Huge tubs of fleshy-leaved shrubs gave a welcoming flash of green.

He turned to look at her, thinking how wonderfully cool she looked with her hair caught back in that sophisticate pleat. Almost aloof—like some exquisite ice maiden. An ice maiden he would one day make take fire, he vowed silently, and then cursed the answering kick of excitement in his loins.

'I have arranged for you to interview both men in the director's office.'

She nodded as she picked up her briefcase from the floor of the car. 'Good. I'll meet you afterwards.'

His smile was bland. 'I don't think you understand, Rose. I will, of course, be present during the interviews—'

'You will not.'

His eyes narrowed with displeasure. 'Quite apart from the fact that I am not used to having my wishes so flagrantly flouted—my family *own* this refinery. Any decisions will ultimately come back to haunt me. I should like to observe each man's interaction with you.'

'Fine.' Rose flashed him a fake-pleasant smile and put her briefcase back down on the floor just as Khalim jumped out of the vehicle and pulled her door open.

'Come on,' he said, seeing that she sat there, so still that she could have been carved from marble.

'I'm not going anywhere.'

Frustration and recognition of that stubborn streak of hers very nearly made him lose his temper. 'Oh, yes, you are,' he contradicted softly. 'I happen to be paying you to—'

'You're paying me to do a job!' she snapped. 'And I cannot do it properly if you happen to be sitting in the room like some great big spectre!'

'Spectre?' he repeated faintly. So she was openly insulting him now, was she?

'You're not just the boss—so to speak—you're their *ruler*, for goodness' sake! How can I expect them to answer me honestly, when all they'll be concerned about is saying what they think *you* want to hear?'

He glowered at her, because he knew she was right—and the only conclusion he could draw from that was that *he* was wrong. And he was never wrong! 'Are you getting out?' he asked dangerously.

'Not unless you agree to my terms,' she answered sweetly.

There was a short, tense silence. He wondered what would happen if he exercised his royal prerogative and picked her up and carried her to the director's private dining room and ravished her there and then? And then shook his head in disbelief at the answering throb of need his thoughts had produced.

Was she going to drive him *insane*, this Rose Thomas?

'Very well,' he agreed tightly. 'It shall be as you wish.'

'Thank you,' she said, but as she slid from the car he caught her wrist, bringing her up close so that black eyes dominated her vision, burning like coals brought up from the depths of hell. And she shivered in response to his touch, even though the temperature was soaring.

'You may find me a far more daunting adversary than you imagine, Rose,' he warned her softly.

Something in his face told her they weren't talking oil refineries now and excitement and fear fused in the pit of her stomach. 'But we aren't fighting any more,' she protested.

'Now you've got your own way, you mean?' he mocked. 'Oh, yes, we are. We've been fighting one way or another since the moment we first met.' And maybe there was only one way to get this confounded conflict out of his system once and for all. He felt another heated tug of desire, provoked by the irresistible darkening of her eyes.

She stared at him. And the stupid thing was that all she wanted right then was for him to kiss her. To kiss her and never stop kissing her. 'K-Khalim?' she said falteringly, shaken by the depths of his anger—an anger which was surely disproportionate to the crime of having the courage to stand up to him? Especially when her professionalism was at stake.

'Come inside,' he said with silky menace as he steeled his heart to the appeal in her eyes, 'and I'll introduce you.'

He showed her into the director's office, which looked like any other high-ranking executive's hidey-hole, with the exception of the pictures on the wall which were both exotic and vaguely erotic. And the desk looked like something out of a museum, with its dark, old wood inlaid with gold.

'Murad Ovezov, the present incumbent, has agreed to speak to you first. He should be able to give you a good idea of what the job entails.'

She hated this new coldness in his eyes, the new *distance* in his attitude towards her. Well, tough! He had hired her to do a job, and do it she would—to the very best of her ability. And that definitely did not include having his powerful and disapproving person present at the interviews!

She gave him a cool smile. 'Thank you, Khalim—you can send him in now.'

It was *unbelievable*, he fumed as he went off to find Murad. She was dismissing him like a servant! She answered him back! Well, she would not be answering him back for much longer. Soon she would be agreeing to everything he said! He would satisfy her as no other man had, and she would be enchained to him for ever!

Murad Ovezov was a man of sixty years, and, although age had painted its inevitable lines around his black eyes, he still exuded a certain *power*. He had worked at the Areeku refinery since it had opened, gradually working his way up until he held the highest position within the factory.

'It's very good of you to see me,' said Rose politely.

He gave a wary bow. 'I was not expecting intervention,' he said, in faultless English.

'I think that you and Khalim have probably decided for yourselves who you wish to replace you.' She smiled, noticing him start when she used the prince's first name. 'I'm here as the fail-safe mechanism—a third party often sees different qualities. Or failures.'

He nodded in comprehension. 'Where would you like to begin?'

She spent half an hour with Murad and then Serdar Kulnuradov was brought in. He was aged forty, confident and knew the refinery inside out. He quoted figures and projections with such fluidity that Rose was left reeling with the breadth of his knowledge.

'Thank you for your time,' she said as he stood up to leave.

Serdar gave a short bow. 'It is my pleasure.' He paused. 'Though it is not usual in Maraban to be interviewed by a woman.'

'Especially a foreign woman?' suggested Rose, with a wry smile. 'I can imagine.'

Oraz Odekov was ushered in next—and a different breed of man entirely. For a start he was aged just thirty and Rose's line of questioning produced quite different answers from those of Serdar.

'And how do you see the future of Areeku?' she asked him at the end of the interview.

And where Serdar had basically said that he wanted more of the same, Oraz was concerned with minimising the effects of pollution.

'You think that's important?' enquired Rose.

'I know so,' he answered simply. 'That is the way of the world today. Countries who do not fight to keep the planet clean will ultimately be discriminated against.'

'Thank you,' she said, and scribbled it down.

He hesitated by the door, and his handsome young face gave a small smile. 'May I be so bold as to say how refreshing it is to have a woman involved in the selection procedure? This, too, is the way forward.'

Go and tell Khalim that, thought Rose irreverently as she smiled back.

Khalim appeared just seconds later. Had he been waiting out in the corridor? thought Rose in wonder. Like a boy waiting outside the headmaster's study.

'Made your mind up?' he asked.

Well, he was certainly to the point when it came to business, thought Rose with some admiration.

'Yes.'

'And?'

'It has to be Oraz.'

There was silence. 'Because he's young and good-looking, I suppose?'

'Please don't insult me, Khalim!'

He sighed. 'Because Serdar is set in older ways than yours and because you are a feminist, is that it, Rose?'

She looked at him steadily. 'I never bring my own personality or prejudices into the selection process—whether or not *I* think I could get on with them is irrelevant. I'm not going to be here, am I? And please don't start calling me a "feminist", Khalim, especially in that derogatory tone.'

'Oh?' His eyes held a mocking challenge. 'You're saying you're not?'

'I'm saying that I don't like labels! Of any kind! I'm just a woman, who believes in equality, that's all.'

The very *last* kind of woman he should be attracted to! And yet he was intelligent enough to realise that her unsuitability was part of what *made* her attractive to him. Her lively mind and keen wit and her refusal to be cowed were qualities he was unused to. Qualities which were proving more aphrodisiac than plump oysters!

'So you're in a dilemma now, aren't you, Khalim?'

He looked at her from between narrowed eyes. Had the minx now managed to read his mind? 'A dilemma?' he stalled.

'Of course. You clearly want Serdar to be the next director, while my advice to you is to appoint Oraz.'

'Because?'

'You want my reasons?'

His smile was coolly assessing. 'That *is* what I'm paying you for.'

She didn't react, but why should she? He spoke nothing but the truth. She *was* here on a professional basis—solely on a professional basis, she reminded herself—and he *was* paying.

'Okay. Serdar has the greater experience, I grant you that, but Oraz has vision. A vision to carry the Areeka well into the middle of this century, and to make it a refinery to be reckoned with.'

He smiled again. 'My very sentiments.'

She stared at him a moment before the gleam in his black

eyes told her exactly what he meant. 'You mean…that you *agree* with me?'

He sighed, almost wishing that she had chosen contrary to his own instincts. 'Yes, Rose. I am entirely in accordance with your wishes.' He glanced at his watch. 'Now let me take you back to the palace for lunch, and afterwards…'

His words tailed off in a silken caress and Rose's heart began to pound uncomfortably in her chest.

'Afterwards?' she asked, relieved that her voice didn't sound *too* eager.

'Afterwards I shall take you riding.'

'I don't ride.'

There was something sensual and uncompromising in his answer.

'But I do,' he said.

CHAPTER EIGHT

THE stables were almost like palaces themselves—huge and cavernous and completely spick and span. Rose knew little of horses, but she knew enough to realise that these bright-eyed animals were well cared for. And that the black stallion whose ear Khalim was tickling—surprisingly gently—was like no other horse she had ever seen, with its fine, narrow body, long legs and slender neck.

'What an unusual creature,' she breathed.

He paused mid-stroke, and Rose found herself wondering what it would be like to have those long, sensuous fingers stroking *her* with such a light caress.

He had changed from his silk robes into close-fitting jodh-purs and a gauzey white shirt, and had borrowed a similar outfit from one of his sisters for Rose. She thought that now he looked like some tousled buccaneer—wild and carefree. Contrasts again, she thought as she watched him.

'This is an Akhal-Teke,' he purred. 'One of the oldest breeds in the world—bred and raced for almost three thousand years. These horses are prized for their desert hardi-ness—with their remarkable endurance and resistance to heat.'

A sense of history and longevity wrapped dreamy arms around her, and her voice was dreamy as she asked, 'And is this *your* horse?'

'Yes, indeed.' His voice deepened with pleasure. 'This is Purr-Mahl. The name means literally, "Full Moon"—'

'And he was born by the light of it, I presume?'

'You presume correctly, Rose.' He smiled. 'I sat and watched the birth, saw the contrast between the silvery-pale

109

gleam of the moon and the night-dark colour of the foal, and I named him there and then. Come, let me sit you upon him.'

'But I don't ride, I told—'

Her protest was already lost on the warm, sultry breeze as he swung her up into his arms, and she wished that he could carry on holding her like that for ever, but he carefully placed her in the saddle instead.

'Press your thighs hard against his body,' he urged and felt a renewed awakening of need. 'Let him know you are there.'

She did as he instructed while he took the reins and led the horse out into the yard where a bodyguard stood, his face inscrutable in the glaring heat of the sun.

Khalim led her round and round the yard for a while and then he murmured something in his own language to the bodyguard, who gave a small bow in response.

Picking up a small leather bag, which he slung over his shoulder, he led her out through the gates to where the stark, shimmering vista of the desert awaited them, with the vast mountains dominating the skyline.

'What did you say to the bodyguard?' she asked him curiously.

'Just that you did not ride, and that I wanted to show you the view from the gate. He is new,' he added casually.

He led the horse a little way into the silvery-white sand, and then suddenly, without warning, he sprang up behind her, and pulled her close into his body at the same time as he seized the reins to urge the horse forward with a murmured word of command and a light slap to the shank.

And they were off!

'Khalim!' Her startled word streamed out like the wind which whipped through her hair.

'Do not be frightened, sweet Rose,' he murmured against her windswept hair.

But it was not fear she felt, it was something far closer to exhilaration. He held her tightly against the hard, lean column of his body, and he handled the horse with such control and mastery that Rose instinctively felt safe.

Safe? Was she mad? Galloping full-pelt across an unforgiving landscape towards the mountains with this dark, enigmatic prince who was taking her who knew where?

Yes, safe. As if this was somehow meant to be. As though all along this had been meant to happen.

As the mountains grew closer, time and distance lost all meaning for her, she had no idea how far they had ridden, or for how long, when, just as suddenly as he'd begun, he steered the horse to a halt in some kind of valley.

Rose could see fig plants and forests of wild walnut trees. And surely down there was the silver glimmer of water?

He jumped down from Purr-Mahl and held his arms up to her and there was a moment of suspended silence while she stared into the enticing glitter of those ebony eyes before sliding down into his arms.

'Sweet Rose,' he said softly.

Had she thought he would kiss her then? Because she was wrong. Instead he took her by the hand and led her towards where she thought she had seen water, and indeed it was, with dense dark thickets of green growing alongside.

He sat down where it looked most hospitable, and patted the ground beside him.

This is a dream, thought Rose. *This is a dream.* And why not? Was Maraban not the land of dreams as well as contrasts?

He pointed to the distant peak of one of the towering mountains.

'When I was a boy,' he said, and his voice softened with memory, 'my father and I used to wait for the first thaw of spring to melt the snow on those mountain peaks, and to flow down to swell the icy river. And we would ride here and drink the crystal waters from a goblet—'

'Why?'

He turned and smiled, and she had never thought that he

could look so impossibly carefree. 'Just for the hell of it.' He shrugged, sounding as English as it was possible to be. He took the leather bag from his shoulder and drew out a small golden goblet, studded with rubies as wine-dark as the robes he had been wearing the other night. 'Always from this goblet.' He smiled.

Rose took it from him and studied it, turning it round in her hands. 'It's very beautiful.'

'Isn't it? Thousands of years ago my ancestors carried it along with many other treasures, when they trekked to this fabled mountain oasis to establish their kingdom.'

But even as he painted beauty with his words, he also painted sadness. For in that moment Rose gleaned some sense of his tradition, his history. He was not as other men. He could not make the same promises as other men. She'd been right from the very first when she had said to Lara that he was not able to offer commitment. And as long as she could accept that…

He put his hand inside the bag again, and drew out a flask in the same gold and claret-coloured jewels as the cup. 'When I was seventeen, he brought me here as usual, only this time we did not drink water; we drank wine.' He smiled. 'Rich, Maraban wine, made from the wild grapevines which grow in the mountain valleys.' His eyes grew soft. 'Will you drink some wine with me, Rose?'

She knew a little then how Eve must have felt when the serpent had offered her the apple, for the question he asked was many-layered. 'I'd love to.'

He tipped some of the ruby liquid into the cup and held it up to her lips. 'Not too much,' he urged gently. 'For Maraban wine is as strong as her men.'

She closed her eyes as she sipped and felt its warm richness invade every pore of her body, and when she opened them again it was to find Khalim staring at her with such a transparent look of hunger on his face that she started, and a droplet of wine trickled from her lips and fell with a splash onto her wrist.

It lay there, a tiny crimson-dark star against the whiteness of her skin and they both stared at it.

'Like blood,' said Khalim slowly. 'The rose has a thorn which draws blood.'

She raised her head and so did he and the look they shared asked and answered the same question, and the goblet fell unnoticed to the ground as he bent his head to kiss her.

Her lips fell open to his velvet touch and she heard herself making a little sound of astonished delight, because she had wanted this for so long. Oh, too long. Much, much too long.

He tangled his fingers in the silken stream of her hair and deepened the kiss. 'Rose,' he groaned against his sweet plunder of her mouth and they fell back against the coarse, desert grass. 'Beautiful, beautiful Rose.'

Her fingers greedily explored the magnificent musculature of his torso through the thin, billowing shirt he wore, kneading her hands against his back as though he were the most delicious kind of dough.

Khalim felt that he might explode with wanting. But more than that—he knew that this woman above all others deserved his honesty. And that had to come now, before it was too late.

He lifted his head from hers and gazed down at her, feeling the heated flush of desire as it snaked its way across his cheekbones. Saw her matching response and the longing which darkened her eyes into twin eclipses.

He drew a long, shuddering breath. 'I have to tell you something,' he began unsteadily.

But Rose was proud. And she was also perceptive—they both knew that. She shook her head. 'I know.'

'You can't know!' he protested.

She wanted to say it *her* way—because she suspected that his words could wound her more deeply than any dagger. 'There can't be any future for us; I know that. This is this, and nothing more than this, and I mustn't read anything else into it.' She actually smiled at his expression of perplexity, recognising that this was a man who was used to calling the shots! 'Don't worry, Khalim,' she finished huskily. 'I won't.'

He shook his head and made a silent curse. By withdrawing emotionally, as she had just done so neatly, she had succeeded in making him want her even more! Impossible! And his need was made all the more poignant by knowing that he could never really have her!

She saw the look of pain etched on his features, and lifted a wondering hand to smooth it down over the hard jut of his jaw. 'Khalim?' she questioned softly. 'What is it?'

He gave a muffled groan as he bent to kiss her neck, his fingers moving to swiftly unbutton her thin shirt, his groan deepening as his hands found and cupped the curved perfection of silk-and lace-covered breasts.

He peeled the shirt open and levered himself up to stare down at her, his eyes as wild and as black as the stallion they had just ridden. He didn't speak another word until he had slithered down the jodhpurs past her ankles and impatiently removed each sock, until she was lying there in just her bra and panties.

'Lace.' He swallowed as his gaze raked from her face, down over her bosom, and down further still until it came to rest with rapt fascination at the flimsy little triangle of silk and lace which was all that kept him from her greatest treasure. 'I always knew you would wear lace, Rose.'

'And you?' She turned the tables as she reached her hand up and scraped her fingernails against his nipples through the white voile of the billowing shirt. 'What about you, Khalim?'

He was used to complete mastery. 'Me?' he questioned unsteadily, an unmistakable note of surprise in his voice. 'What about me, Rose?'

'Take it off,' she ordered softly.

Her words sent the blood coursing heatedly around his veins. 'Is that a...command?' he demanded unsteadily.

She revelled in the sense that something here was different for him. 'It most certainly is.'

The sight of her head pillowed on the flaxen satin of her hair, and her big blue eyes and soft pouting mouth, was almost as much of a turn-on as her near-naked body. Khalim began to unbutton his shirt with fingers which threatened to tremble.

'You have me in your thrall, sweet Rose—see how my hands shake,' he murmured as the shirt was flung onto the desert scrub. 'Now name your next command.'

'Take it off,' she instructed, revelling in the heady sensation of having such power over this man. *This* man.

'What?' But the attempted tease came out in a kind of strangled plea.

'Everything.'

His long black riding boots were kicked off, and then he fingered the button of his jodhpurs, seeing from the automatic thrusting of her breasts that she was hurtling towards a stage of almost unbearable excitement. You and me both, he thought, with a helpless kind of rapture.

He made his undressing as slow and as deliberate as he could, and Rose was shocked, startled and unbearably aroused to see that he wore nothing beneath the jodhpurs, absolutely nothing. Nothing to disguise the awesome power of his erection. She swallowed, wondering whether... whether...

He read the expression in her eyes as the jodhpurs joined the shirt. 'You worry that I am too much of a man for you?'

She laughed in soft delight at the arrogant boast. 'Maybe you worry that I am too much of a woman for you!'

For answer he pulled her panties down with more speed than grace, and then his hand reached behind her to unclip her bra with one deft movement, freeing the tumultuous splendour of her breasts.

He took one breathless look at her nakedness, before coming to lie on top of her, dipping his head to suckle greedily at her breasts, his fingers moving between her thighs to flick at her slick heat.

Rose's head fell back. 'Oh! Khalim!'

'You want me to stop?' he suggested, lifting his head away from her nipple so that she almost fainted with disappointment.

'Yes! No!'

'What, then?'

'I want to savour it. Savour you.' She wanted this feeling to go on and on and on and never stop. Khalim *hers*, in her arms, as she had dreamed of him being since the moment she had first seen him.

'Next time,' he promised. 'This has been too long in the waiting. Now we will satisfy our hunger—later we will attend to the feast.'

She felt the caress of his fingers and shuddered. 'This is feast enough, Khalim.' She sighed. 'Feast enough.'

'Oh, Rose.' He smiled as her body responded instinctively to his touch. 'Sweet, beautiful Rose.'

But he could wait no longer, his desire for her too intense to bear. In that moment just before the communion of their bodies, he felt as though he were about to embrace life in a way in which he had never embraced it before.

He parted her thighs with eager hands and she felt the unbelievable power of him moving against her. Surely it was too soon? Surely she was not ready? But she dissolved into honeyed heat at just that first touch, and her thighs parted wider of their own accord and as he took one long, sweet thrust he made a low moan.

He filled her in every way he could—physically, mentally, emotionally. Joined in a fundamental flow, while the hot desert sun beat down on them, he was no longer Prince Khalim and she no longer Rose Thomas, the woman of his employ. Now he was just a man, and she was just a woman, locked in the most basic rhythm of all.

She couldn't remember the kisses, or the murmured things

he whispered in her ear—some in English and some in a far more thrilling foreign tongue which she recognised as Marabanese. She only knew that the stars were beckoning her, that her world was about to explode.

And his.

He lifted his head to stare down at her, as helpless at that moment as he had ever been, sensing her release in conjunction with his own.

And then it happened, on and on and on, until their cries were replaced by the soft sound of the desert wind, their stricken breathing calming at last and their sweat-sheened bodies glued together.

Rose felt her eyelids drifting downwards, but he shook her awake.

'No, Rose,' he murmured. 'You must not sleep.'

'*Must* not?' she questioned automatically, even as a lazy yawn escaped her.

He smiled, but it was a rueful smile. Even in the midst of their mutual pleasure—still she challenged him! He kissed his finger and placed it over her lips to silence her. 'They will come for us very soon,' he said.

That had her sitting up immediately, and she saw his eyes darken at the unfettered movement of her bare breasts. 'Who will? When?'

'My bodyguards.' He shrugged, leaning over to rescue her discarded panties and bra.

She shook the stray grains of sand out of her underwear and turned to glare at him. 'And they'll know where to find you, of course?' she demanded crossly. 'This is the usual location for your little *trysts*, is it?'

'Rose, Rose, Rose,' he murmured. 'Fiery, beautiful, argumentative Rose! I have never brought a woman here before—'

No, of course he hadn't. No other Western woman had ever accompanied him to Maraban. And no Maraban woman would have cavorted with such abandon on the ground with the heir to the throne.

'How will they find us, then?' She stood up and pulled her panties all the way over her slender thighs, enjoying the brief look of frustration which clouded his eyes. 'Are they clairvoyant, or something?'

He zipped up his jodhpurs with difficulty. Impossible that she should have aroused him again so quickly, but somehow...somehow, she had. 'They will follow the trail of the horse,' he said shortly, and roughly pulled his shirt on.

Rose was struggling into her clothes. 'What must I look like?' she moaned. 'Won't they take one look at us and know exactly what we've been doing?'

He gave a rueful shrug. Rose cherished honesty, didn't she? Then honesty she would have. 'They would take one look at you and think that I was the worst kind of fool if we had *not* been doing what they suppose.'

'Oh!' Her cheeks were burning. 'And what will they think of me?'

He gave her a cool, steady look. 'Do you seek the approval of my bodyguards?' he questioned. 'Or my approval?'

'Neither!' she snapped. 'I'm thinking about my professional reputation!'

'But your job is done. You are here now as my guest. My *lover*.' He lingered on the last word with a sense of treasures to come, and then looked at her with a question glittering from his black eyes. Would she voice her objection to the term of possession without any promise of commitment?

But Rose simply stared back at him without regrets. She had given herself to him freely. Completely. In a way she had given herself to no man before. She had never known that love-making could be that intense, that profound, that...*fundamental*. She shivered with the memory.

And he had not told her lies. On the contrary, he had been totally open with her. Had told her before he'd made love to her that there could be no long-term future—and she had accepted that and given herself to him as he had given himself to her.

So why not enjoy these exotic fruits of temptation for as long as they were available? To treasure and store up memories which would see her into old age. For she knew without a doubt that no man could ever follow Khalim.

'Will you be my lover, Rose?' he asked softly.

She opened her mouth to speak just as she heard the dry beat of hooves on the sand, and looked up into the distance to see four horsemen on the horizon, galloping fast towards them.

And then she smiled, deliberately enticing him with a slanted look of remembered pleasure. 'Yes, Khalim. I will be your lover.'

CHAPTER NINE

ROSE felt as though she had been taken prisoner on the ride back to the Palace.

There had been a short, sharp exchange between Khalim and a man she had never seen before, a formidable-looking man in rich robes, whose bearing immediately distinguished him as someone of substance. Rose couldn't understand a word of what they were saying, but she guessed that the man's quietly restrained anger was an admonishment to Khalim for breaching security.

Khalim lifted her gently onto his mount and she held on tightly to his waist, longing to turn her head and to steal a glance at him, but she resisted, relieved when the golden gleam of the palace came into view.

Khalim dismounted and lifted her down, and in one single, suspended moment their eyes met and in his she read, what…?

Longing. Yes. And surely a brief dazzle of tenderness. But something else, too—something which stirred a wistful fear deep inside her—for wasn't that regret there? A regret which told as clearly as words would have done that she must accept the limitations of their affair. And never hope.

'I'll see you to your rooms,' he said in a low voice.

The man in the rich robes said something and Khalim turned his head and made a snapped reply.

'Come!' he said to Rose, and led her through the courtyard and into the palace.

'Who was that man?' she asked him once they were out of earshot.

'My cousin, Raschid,' he said.

'He's angry with you?'

Khalim allowed himself a small smile. 'Furious,' he agreed. But making love to Rose had been worth any amount of fury.

'And will you get into trouble?'

He raised his dark brows. 'I think not. I am the prince, after all,' he said autocratically.

He spoke with an arrogance that no other man could have got away with, thought Rose, guiltily acknowledging the thrill of pleasure that his mastery gave her. 'Of course you are,' she murmured.

They reached her rooms and he paused, reaching his hand out to cup her chin, wanting to kiss her above all else, and to lay her body bare once more. He bit down the dull ache of frustration.

'I will have food sent to you here for I cannot be with you this evening,' he told her shortly.

She opened her eyes very wide as her heart pounded with disappointment, but she was damned if she would let it show. 'That's a pity,' she said calmly.

A *pity*? Had he thought she would beg him to stay? Or interrogate him about where he was going? And didn't her lack of jealousy make him want her all the more? 'But I will come to you later, sweet Rose.'

'I might be asleep.'

'Then I will wake you,' he said on a silken promise, and he planted a sweet, hard kiss on her mouth before sweeping away.

Rose slowly got out of her rumpled clothes and took a long, scented bath before slipping into a pair of pure white trousers made out of finest cotton-lawn, and a little shirt of the same material.

Fatima appeared with a tempting array of food—a type of tomato stew with baby okra and lamb accompanied by a jewel-coloured rice dish. And a platter of pastries, glistening with syrup and stuffed with nuts and raisins. There was pomegranate juice and mint tea to drink.

But once she had gone, Rose only picked uninterestedly at the dishes on offer.

How could she concentrate on something as mundane as food, when her mind and her senses were filled with the memory of Khalim and his exquisite love-making? He had been everything. Tender and yet fierce. His kisses passionate and cajoling. He had moaned aloud in her arms, had not held back on showing her his pleasure—and that in itself felt like a small victory.

With disturbing clarity she recalled the vision of their limbs entwined, his so dark and so muscular, contrasting almost indecently with her own milky-white skin, and then she sighed, wondering if she would ever be able to concentrate on anything other than her Marabanesh prince ever again.

More as diversion therapy than anything else, she picked up Robert Cantle's book on Maraban, and read the chapter on Khalim's forefathers, and the establishment of the mountain kingdom.

There were richly painted portraits of his recent ancestors—and one in particular which had her scanning the page avidly. Malik the Magnificent, she read. It was him! Khalim's great-great-grandfather whose thwarted love had borne such a striking and uncanny resemblance to Rose herself.

She studied a face almost as proudly handsome as Khalim's with its hard, sculpted contours and those glittering black eyes and luscious lips, and she sighed again. Don't start getting all hopeful, Rose, she told herself fiercely. You could not have had it spelt out more explicitly that love affairs like this have no future.

At eleven, she put the book down, telling herself that he would not come tonight. She began pulling the brush through her hair, telling herself not to be angry, but she *was* angry. Was this a taste of things to come? How he thought he could treat his women? Keep them hanging around *at his convenience*?

She flung the hairbrush down just as the door slowly

opened, and there stood Khalim in robes of deepest sapphire, his eyes narrowing with undisguised hunger as he caught the unmistakable outline of her body through the thin material of her clothes.

Rose bristled. 'I didn't hear you knock.'

'That's because I didn't,' he said, shutting the door softly behind him.

'Why not?'

He stilled as he heard the reprimand in her voice, and he turned to meet the blue blaze of accusation which spat from her eyes. 'Because we are now lovers, Rose. This afternoon you gave yourself to me with an openness which suggested that we have no need for barriers between us. Do I need to knock on your door?'

The voice of reason in her head told her to back off, but she had missed him, wanted him, and felt hurt by his unexplained disappearance, and so she ignored it. 'Damned right you need to knock!' she retorted. 'I may be mature enough to realise that this is a very grown-up affair with no promises or expectations on either side—but that does not mean that I'm prepared to be trampled on like some sort of chattel!'

If he hadn't wanted her so much, he would have walked out there and then. No woman had ever spoken to him with such a flagrant lack of respect—especially when he had had her gasping and sighing in his arms on the desert grass!

'I do not treat you as a chattel,' he answered coldly.

'No? You just make love to me and then waltz off for the evening without bothering to tell me where you are going?'

He hid a smile. Ah! So she was *jealous*, was she? Good! 'But you just told me that neither of us have any expectations, Rose,' he demurred.

'That's not an expectation!' she declared wildly, wondering where all her powers of logic had flown to. 'That's just simple courtesy. Where were you?'

He had been foolish to imagine that he would not have to tell her. He had not wanted to hurt her, but now he saw that by not telling her he must have hurt her more. He was not used to analysing what effect his actions would have on a woman's feelings. Usually, he did what the hell he liked, and was allowed to get away with it. With anything.

'I had dinner with my mother and my father,' he said softly. 'My father is too frail to accommodate—' he very nearly said 'strangers' but bit the word back in time '—guests,' he finished heavily.

Rose stared at him. 'And that's all? Why didn't you tell me that?'

She would never be able to find out, and yet Khalim realised that if he was anything less than truthful with his fiery Rose, he would lose her.

'No, that isn't all.' He sighed. 'There was a young woman there, too.'

Rose froze as some new and unknown danger shimmered into her subconscious. 'I'm not sure that I understand what you mean.'

'My father is very frail—'

'I know that.'

'Soon he will die,' he said starkly, and there was a long, heavy pause. 'And I must take a bride when the year of mourning is complete.'

It was the most pain she had ever felt and she felt like smashing something—anything—but somehow, miraculously, she managed to keep her face composed. Why crumple when this was what her instincts and her common sense should have told her? 'And this—young woman—was, I presume, one of the *suitable* candidates being lined up for you?'

How preposterous it sounded coming from his beautiful, English Rose! 'Yes.' He thought back to the girl being brought in by her mother, her slim, young body swathed in the finest embroidered silks. Only her eyes had been visible, and very beautiful eyes they had been, too—huge, and doe-like, the deep rich colour of chocolate.

But she had been tongue-tied at first, and then so docile

and submissive—so adoring of her prince and heir. He had seen his mother's approving nod, and the sharp look of pleasure on the face of the girl's mother, and had tried to imagine being married to a woman such as this.

She would bear him fine Marabanesh sons and in time she would grow fat and he would grow bored. Had his mother and his father noticed his distraction with the idea? he wondered now.

'So is she going to be the lucky one?' asked Rose, only just preventing herself from snarling.

'No, she is not.'

'Oh? Did she discover how you'd spent your afternoon, then? Lying with me under the hot desert sun? Making love to *me*?'

The taunt triggered memory, fused and exploded in a fury of anger and almost unbearable passion. He pulled her roughly into his arms, though he saw from the instant dilation of her eyes that she was not objecting. Not objecting one bit, he thought as he drove his mouth down hard on hers.

And only when he had slaked a little of his hunger for her did he lift his head and gaze down into her dazed face as her eyelids fluttered open to stare up at him.

Her lips opened to frame his name, but no word came.

'Rose,' he said gently, his breath warm and soft on her face. 'How can we be lovers if you make such unreasonable demands on me?'

Her fingers bit into the hard strength of his shoulders beneath the sapphire silk. 'Most people wouldn't call them unreasonable!'

'Most people, most people,' he chided. 'Rose, Rose, my sweetest Rose—I am not most people. We both know that. I told you that right from the very beginning.'

She shook her head sadly. 'No, not right from the beginning, Khalim. You told me just before you made love to me, when making love had become as inevitable as night following day. You did everything in your not inconsiderable power to get me to arrive at that point. You played me as you would—' memory flashed into her subconscious as she recalled something he had told her about his schooldays, his love of fishing '—a *fish*! That's what you did! Yes, you did, and don't deny it! Teased me and tempted me, and—'

He cut short her protests with a forefinger placed softly on her lips, feeling them tremble beneath his touch, and he felt a surge of something far greater than mere desire. How well she knew him! How was this possible in so short a time?

'Yes, I plead guilty to your accusations,' he admitted slowly. 'Every one of them.'

Her anger was mollified by the triumph of knowing that she understood him a little too much for his liking, and her fingertips curled spontaneously into the nape of his neck, like a kitten's claws.

He felt her capitulation in the instinctive sway of her body, her hips folding into his, where fire and desire were building and burning, and he groaned.

'So can we not just enjoy this…now, my sweet, sweet Rose? To take what many pleasures are ours?'

It was, she recognised, an expression of need as much as lust, and the closest that Khalim would ever come to…not begging, exactly, because a man like Khalim would never, ever beg. But beseeching, certainly. She stared up into his face, and all her objections withered into dust.

'Yes, my darling,' she said shakily. 'We can.'

His hand was unsteady as he traced a slow line with his finger, from neck to navel, the filmy white material of her blouse moulding itself to the slim curves beneath.

'I want to see you naked,' he said huskily. 'Properly naked against satin, not sand.' He drew the cotton top over her head, his breath freezing with pleasure as he saw the unfettered lushness of her breasts and the flaxen hair which streamed down over them. He bent his head to kiss one puckered, rosy nipple.

'Oh!' she sighed, squirming her hips in helpless pleasure. 'You are a wicked, wicked man, Khalim.'

'You bring out the wickedness in me,' he murmured.

'The feeling is mutual,' she murmured back. 'So, so mutual.' Rose's hands slid underneath the sapphire silk of his gown, fingertips feasting on the feel of the satin skin which lay over the muscular definition of his torso. She felt him shudder beneath her touch and knew another moment of triumph, suspecting that once again he was close to the edge. And that was a heady feeling. This man of control and power—*hers*!

'I wanted to make this a long, slow undressing,' he said, bending his head to whisper in her ear.

'I sense a ''but'' coming.'

'Mmm. I think it will take many days before I can bear to prolong the pleasure in that way. Shall we...?' He paused, and trickled a finger down to rest possessively in the small dip of her navel. 'Shall we quickly remove these constraining garments, so that we can come together without barrier?'

But the word stirred an uncomfortable thought which had occurred to him over dinner that very night.

'And I have brought with me—' he scowled as he forced himself to say the abhorrent word, but only abhorrent when used in connection with Rose '—*condoms*! We were too reckless and too hungry for one another earlier.' When, for the first time in his life, he had made love without protection. It had also occurred to him that she might have become pregnant, and an intense and primitive yearning had swept over him. Only to be replaced by a fervent prayer that it should not be so.

For it would be impossible if Rose Thomas were carrying his child. Impossible!

Rose shrugged the slippery silk impatiently over his shoulders and let it flutter to the ground.

'You don't need them,' she told him.

Black eyes iced instantly at the implication. 'What don't I need?' he questioned softly.

She met his gaze without flinching. 'Condoms. We won't need them.' She hesitated. Surely she wouldn't have to spell it out for a man of the world such as this?

'Why not?'

Apparently she did.

'I'm on the pill,' she said bluntly.

'No!' His mouth formed the denial as if he had been stung.

'Yes,' she insisted quietly.

His heart pounding with an unendurable jealousy, he tightened his grip on her. 'So this is the way of Western women, is it?' he demanded. 'Always prepared, is that so? *Just in case?*'

'Don't be so hypocritical, Khalim,' she answered with dignity. 'I happen to be on the pill because my periods were heavy and irregular—'

'Your *periods*?' he demanded incredulously.

She guessed correctly that women did not speak of such matters with Khalim. So they were allowed certain intimacies with him such as sex, were they? But nothing in the way of *real* intimacy. Of women as they really were. Well, she had taken him on *his* terms; now let him take her on *hers*. She tried to make allowances for his upbringing and his culture. 'It's a very effective remedy,' she explained patiently.

'And also very convenient if you happen to just want to fall into bed with someone?' he scorned.

She wrenched herself away from him and fixed him with a withering stare. 'If you believe *that*, then you can get out of here right now, and don't bother coming back!'

He could see from the fire in her blue eyes that she meant it, and he forced himself to draw a steadying breath. 'I shouldn't have said that—'

'No, you're right—you shouldn't!' Her breathing came fast and rapid and indignant. 'How many lovers have you slept with in your life, Khalim?'

'You dare to ask me *that*?' he questioned dangerously.

'I'll bet it's a whole lot more than *I* have—which is precisely *two!*'

He flinched again and his mouth hardened. How dared there have been another before him? How *dared* there! *'Two!'*

'Yes, two. Actually not terribly shocking considering that I'm twenty-seven years old and have grown up in the kind of culture I have! I have *never* gone to bed with anyone indiscriminately! Can you look me in the eye and honestly say that *you* haven't, either?'

He stared at her, torn between fury and admiration. His beautiful, logical Rose! Applying the same rules of life for her as well as him! He bit down the pain of jealousy and a slow light began to glimmer at the back of the black eyes.

'You have never actually been to bed with *me* either, have you, sweet Rose?' he murmured, taking her unresisting hand and raising it to his lips to kiss it. 'And I think that is a situation which we should remedy now, with all seemly haste.'

How powerful he looked. How masterfully dark and virile and proud. Rose wondered half wildly whether she should have prevented him from scooping her up into his arms and carrying her over to the low mattress. A victor with his spoils, she thought weakly.

But then she was the victor, too. Because to have provoked that look of sensual promise coupled with a barely restrained impatience to make love to her was the most potent sensation she had ever encountered.

She let the last of her misgivings go as he laid her down on the embroidered coverlet, tugging at the silk cord which bound his loose trousers so they fell to the floor.

My heavens, but he was aroused! Darkly and magnificently aroused. Her mouth began to tremble as he slid her cotton trousers all the way down her legs and tossed them aside with an impatient disdain.

'Khalim,' she gasped as he came to lie beside her, his arms snaking possessively around her waist while his eyes burned down at her like smouldering coal.

'What is it, sweetest Rose? You want me to kiss you now?'

It was exactly what she wanted—the touch and the warmth and the security of his lips caressing hers. So that for one mad and crazy moment she could imagine that it was not lust which made this kiss such magic, but fool herself into thinking it was something as elusive and as precious as love.

CHAPTER TEN

KHALIM stayed with her for most of the night, but slipped out as dawn began to paint a pink and golden light on the horizon.

He swiftly dressed, then bent his head to kiss her, his lips lingering regretfully on her pouting mouth. 'The plane leaves at midday,' he murmured. 'Be ready to leave at ten.'

'Mmm?' she questioned groggily.

It had been the night of her life. His love-making had known no boundaries—nor hers, either. She'd given herself to him without inhibition. But with love, she realised with a sinking heart as she acknowledged the emotion which had first crept and then exploded deep inside her.

She loved him.

The realisation gave her no real pleasure—for what pleasure could ever be gained from a love which was doomed right from the start? But she *had* taken him on her terms, and she *did* want him, and because of that she pinned a sleepy smile onto her face.

'Mmm?' she questioned again, stalling for time, time to be able to react in the way expected of her, and not with the gnawing feeling of insecurity which had started to overwhelm her every time she thought about losing him.

'Be ready by ten,' he instructed softly, wishing that he could lie with her here until the morning sun filtered its way in precious golden shafts through the shutters.

She nodded and watched him go, all elegance and grace as he swished out of the room in the silken robes.

She ate the fruit and bread which Fatima brought to her room for breakfast and was ready by nine when there was a knock on the door and she opened it to find Khalim standing there, changed from his robes into one of his impeccably cut suits, ready for the flight back to London, and with an unusual expression on his face.

He looked perplexed.

'What is it?' she asked him quickly.

He shrugged. 'My father has requested that he meet you.'

Rose opened the door a little wider. 'You sound surprised.'

He was. Exceedingly. It was inconceivable—to *his* mind, in any case—that his father should express a wish to meet his Western blonde. But he would not tell Rose that.

'He is so frail,' he told her truthfully, 'that he sees few visitors.'

Except for prospective brides, thought Rose bitterly—bet he sees *loads* of those. 'Then I must be honoured,' she answered.

He nodded absently, his mind far away. 'I will arrange to have your bags taken out to the car,' he said. 'Now, come with me.'

She thought how distracted he seemed as he led her through the maze of marble corridors into a much larger and grander part of the palace. Past silent figures who watched them with black eyes which were unreadable, until at last an elaborately ornate door was flung open and they were ushered into a bedchamber.

At the far end of the room was a large and lavishly decorated bed, and, lying on it, a man whose unmoving rigidity proclaimed the severity of his illness.

'Come,' said Khalim softly.

By his father's bed sat his mother, her face troubled, and she nodded briefly at Khalim and then, not quite so briefly, at Rose.

'Father,' said Khalim. 'This is Rose Thomas.'

In a face worn thin by illness, only the eyes remained living and alert. Keen, black eyes, just like his son's. He gave a small smile and Rose was overwhelmed by the graciousness of that smile.

'So,' he said slowly. 'I believe that I must thank you for confirming Khalim's chosen successor for the oil refinery.' Another smile, this time rather more rueful. 'An opinion which differed from my own. And therefore Khalim said that we must bring in an independent arbitrator to decide.'

Rose looked up at Khalim in surprise, and met a mocking glance in return.

'Thank you. It is a great honour to meet you, sir,' she said quietly, and bowed her head.

The old man nodded and said something very rapid to Khalim, in Marabanese, and then Khalim tapped her arm. 'Come, Rose,' he said. 'Will you wait in the outer chamber while I bid my father farewell?'

Rose slipped silently from the room, her heart clenching as she read the pain in Khalim's face. Did every departure seem like the last time he would ever see his father? she wondered as she sat on a low couch outside the bedchamber.

It seemed a long time before Khalim came out again, and when he did his face was grave and Rose sprang to her feet.

'Is everything…okay?' she asked. It seemed a stupid question under the circumstances, but Khalim did not seem to notice.

'His physician is with him now,' he said slowly. 'Come, Rose—we must go to the airport, where the plane awaits us.'

They walked back along the corridor and he glanced down at her. 'The way you looked at me back there,' he mused.

Rose's eyes opened very wide. Had he seen the tell-tale signs of love? she worried. And wouldn't that be enough to send him fleeing in the opposite direction?

'When?'

'When my father told you that we had agreed to bring in an outsider to arbitrate, you looked surprised. What was the matter, Rose—did you imagine that I had invented the job as a ploy to get you out to Maraban?'

'It would sound insufferably arrogant of me to say yes,'

she answered slowly. 'But maybe just a little, then, yes—yes, perhaps I did.'

He admired her honesty—it would have been easy for her to have been evasive, and to lie. And, in truth, had not such a vacancy existed—then might he *not* have manufactured an excuse to bring her on such a trip? He smiled. 'You have fulfilled all my expectations, Rose. In every way and more.'

The limousine whisked them to the airport at Dar-gar and they were immediately escorted onto the plane, where Philip Caprice and the two glamorous air stewardesses were waiting for them.

And it wasn't until the plane had taken off into a cloudless blue sky and Khalim found his eyes wandering irresistibly to her pure, beautiful profile that he began to experience some of the misgivings which his father had already expressed so eloquently.

He had not wanted to leave her this morning, and now he felt like dismissing Philip and making love to her again. Rose Thomas was getting under his skin, he acknowledged—and he seemed to be hell-bent on breaking every single rule which mattered.

His mouth hardening, he deliberately picked up his brief-case and pulled a sheaf of papers out.

Rose interpreted the body language. The almost impercep-tible way he turned away from her. Oh, yes! He'd been vir-tually silent in the car on the way to the airport, and now she was getting the cold freeze. Was he having second thoughts? Had he thought more about the heinous crime of her being on the pill and decided that she was the worst kind of woman?

Was this the reality of being Khalim's temporary woman?

She got to her feet and met the hard, dark question in his eyes. 'I'm going to freshen up,' she said, and picked up the smaller of her two bags.

When she emerged a whole half an hour later, Khalim froze.

While in Maraban she had dressed most appropriately, in trousers or long skirts—clothes which modestly concealed her delectable shape. But now she had changed into a strappy little sundress in a golden colour which matched her hair, and which showed off far more brown and shapely leg than he was comfortable with.

He shifted in his seat. Not at *all* comfortable with. He waited until she had decorously taken her place beside him before challenging her.

'What is the meaning of this?'

She turned her head and raised her eyebrows. Now he was *talking* to her as though she were his concubine! 'The meaning of what?'

'This...this...vulgar *display* of your body,' he grated, realising that he did not want her body on show for anyone. Anyone but *him*!

'But this is exactly the kind of dress I was wearing when we first met,' she pointed out reasonably. 'You liked it well enough then, as I remember.'

'But now,' he said coolly, 'I do not.'

'Oh?'

He lowered his voice to a sultry whisper. 'I do not want other men looking at you in that way!'

'You mean the way *you're* looking at me?' she enquired innocently.

'That is *different!*''

'I fail to see how!' she answered wilfully.

He drummed his fingers impatiently against the arm rest. Well, short of marching her back into the bathroom and insisting that she put something decent on, there was little he could do.

He made a terse and impatient sound beneath his breath, feeling the uncharacteristic tug of frustration—and not solely sexual frustration, either. No, this was a frustration born out of the knowledge that he had finally met a woman who would not bend to his will! His match!

'Wear what you like!' he gritted.

'I intend to!'

The rest of the journey was completed in a stony silence, while Rose fumed and wondered how she could ever have thought herself in love with such a tyrant of a man.

Then she stole a glance at that beautiful, dark profile and thought of his tenderness and his passion during the night, and once again her heart pained her as though someone had driven a stiletto into it, then slowly twisted it round.

By the time they had disembarked into the waiting limousine at Heathrow Airport, Khalim was in the rare quandary of not knowing what to do. Or, rather, of knowing exactly what he *wanted* to do—which was to rush Miss Rose Thomas straight back to his suite at the Granchester Hotel and ravish her to within an inch of her life. So that for ever after she would comply with every demand he ever made!

He sighed. The trouble was—that he did not want that at all. Her fire and her independence inspired him almost as much as it frustrated him. What a hollow victory it would be to have Rose in the compliant position he usually expected of his women!

The car slowed as it approached the busy thoroughfares of London and he forced himself to look at her.

Forced, indeed! As if looking at her could give him nothing but untold pleasure!

'Would you like to come home with me?' he murmured.

For Khalim, he sounded almost biddable, Rose thought. But not quite.

'You mean to the Granchester?' she enquired coolly.

'Of course!'

She shook her head. She had had enough of his surroundings and their influence. 'Why don't you come back with me?' she questioned innocently.

To that flat she shared with the other girl? Unthinkable!

And then he thought of the alternative, which was even more unthinkable—that he went home without her!

'Very well,' he answered.

'There's no need to make it sound as though I'm leading you into the lion's cage!' said Rose crossly.

'Not a lion, no,' he agreed, a hint of humour lightening the night-dark eyes. 'More some beautiful and graceful cat!'

She wasn't sure whether it really *was* a compliment—but she found herself basking in it anyway.

But as the car began to approach her road, Rose began to wonder whether it had been such a good idea to invite him. What if Lara had a load of her out-of-work actor friends around, lying all over the place and drinking wine and smoking cigarettes?

Or what if Lara had had a heavy night, and had left the place in a state of disarray—a common enough occurrence when Rose wasn't around to tidy up after her.

They left the bodyguard sitting in the car outside and went upstairs to the flat.

It was rather better than Rose had anticipated, but not much. There weren't a *crowd* of Lara's friends—just her on-off boyfriend, Giles, whom Rose always thought of as *very* off.

Giles had been born into a wealthy family, imagining that the world owed him a living. He had fluked his way into drama school and then coasted through the course—only just managing not to be asked to leave by the skin of his teeth.

Unfortunately he had the kind of blond-haired, blue-eyed looks and carved aristocratic cheekbones which meant that he could get any woman that he wanted—and Lara wanted him far more than he wanted her.

Which meant, thought Rose grimly, that she waited on him as if he were an invalid. Cooking up various little treats for him and pouring him glasses of wine at all hours of the day.

Like now.

So why was he polishing off a glass of Chardonnay in the middle of the afternoon? And looking at Khalim with a kind of jealous incredulity.

But then, Rose decided with more than a little satisfaction, Giles rarely met men who transcended *his* good looks so completely!

She looked around at the plates and cups and wineglasses littered around the sitting room and saw Khalim's lips curve with undisguised displeasure. Well, *let* him judge her, she thought proudly as she bent to pick up an empty wine bottle which was in danger of tripping someone up!

'Lara, you've already met Khalim,' she said shortly. 'Khalim, I don't believe you've met Giles, who is Lara's—'

'Lover,' drawled Giles arrogantly.

Khalim's facial muscles didn't move an inch. 'It is my pleasure,' he said smoothly and looked at Rose with a question in his eyes.

Now what? thought Rose helplessly. Did she take him to her room? No, she couldn't—she just *couldn't*. Not with Giles smirking like that and Lara affecting that puppy-dog expression whenever she looked at Khalim.

'Would you like some coffee?' she asked weakly.

'Thank you,' he replied, without enthusiasm.

The kitchen looked as though someone had tried to start World War Three in there—with every surface covered in used crockery and glasses.

And Lara had used up all the real coffee, thought Rose in disbelief as she picked up a nearly-empty jar and held it up to him.

'Is instant okay?' she questioned.

'Instant?' he echoed, as though she had just started speaking in Marabanese.

'Coffee,' she elaborated.

'Do you have any tea?'

'Yes. Yes, I do.' She made them two cups of herb tea and then cleared the table so that they could sit down and drink it.

They sat facing one another warily across the rising steam from their cups.

Now what? thought Rose again, before getting back some of her customary spirit.

'You don't *have* to stay, you know,' she bristled.

'No, I don't,' he agreed calmly, thinking that Rose—*his* Rose—should not have to live amidst such outrageous chaos. 'But you will not come back with me to the Granchester either, will you?'

'No.'

'Do you mind telling me why?'

How to explain that his costly surroundings only emphasised their inequality, and that if she was to spend the tenure of their fragile relationship always on *his* territory, then it would always seem a little tainted.

'Can't we just be like a normal couple?' she demanded. 'I don't always want to be surrounded by your bodyguards and the awe in which people hold you. Everyone always defers to your status—it's always there. A barrier.' She nearly said, A barrier towards getting to know you, and then stopped herself. Maybe he didn't *want* to get to know her on the level she craved to discover him.

He stared across the table at her. 'Then we seem to have reached some kind of stalemate, don't we, Rose? What do you suggest?'

The idea hit her like a thunderclap. If only they *could* be an 'ordinary' couple. The idea grew. 'Why don't you rent a flat of your own?' she suggested. 'A flat where we can meet as equals?'

'A *flat*?' he repeated.

'Why, yes.' Of course, they would never be *quite* the same as a normal couple. Khalim would never have to go begging to the bank manager for a loan, for example. But neutral territory would give them some kind of equality, surely?

'There are loads of—' she forced herself to say the hateful word '—short-let flats on the market in London. Furnished or unfurnished—suit yourself. Wouldn't it be…nice…' she gave him a kind of feline smile '…to have a place where we were free to be ourselves? Within reason, of course,' she added hastily. 'Obviously there would have to be some provision for your bodyguard.'

He raised his eyebrows. Good of her! And then he thought about it. And thought some more. Didn't her words have more than a kernel of truth in them? Wouldn't a rented flat give him a fleeting kind of freedom? The kind of freedom which most men of his age took for granted? The freedom…and he swallowed as he imagined a whole place of their own. Where Rose could wander around wearing what she wanted.

Where they could watch a video and eat their supper lolling around on a sofa, as he had seen his friend Guy do with Sabrina on so many occasions.

'Very well.' He nodded, and his mind started ticking over. 'I can see the wisdom behind your idea. I will get Philip to start looking immediately—'

'No, Khalim!' she said, interrupting him. 'You have to do it like other people do! *You* go and look at flats. You find the one you want and *you* do all the transactions. Do it yourself for once! Forget Philip!'

Her feisty challenge drove the blood heatedly around his veins and in that moment his desire to possess her made him feel almost dizzy. But he would have to wait. He would not bed her here with the feckless actor and her sweet but rather untidy flatmate listening to them.

'I most certainly will, Rose,' he promised. 'And with haste.' He lowered his voice into a sensual whisper. 'Because believe me when I tell you that I cannot bear to wait for you much longer.'

CHAPTER ELEVEN

IT WAS not a flat, of course. It was a magnificent, four-storey house in Chelsea.

'A flat would have caused too many problems for my security,' explained Khalim as he showed her through a wealth of magnificent, high-ceilinged rooms. And his Head of Security still had not forgiven him his breach when he had galloped off across the desert sand with Rose locked tightly against him! 'So what do you think?' he murmured. 'Does my Rose approve?'

How could she do anything but? Rose let her gaze travel slowly around the main drawing room. Everywhere she looked she could see yellow and blue flowers—saffron roses and lemon freesias, and the splayed indigo fingers of iris—and she was reminded of the bouquet he had sent her, when he'd first been trying to...

To what? To seduce her? She turned her head, so that he could not see her eyes. Had that been his only intention? Maybe it had, she acknowledged, but something else had grown from that intent. You didn't share a house with a woman if sex was the only thing on your mind.

Oh, *stop* it, Rose, she remonstrated with herself. Stop playing Little Miss Wistful.

'I love it. It's beautiful,' she said, and hoped that her voice didn't *sound* too wistful. Because they were *playing* house, not setting up house together, and she must never let herself forget that. But at times like this it wasn't easy.

She stared in slight awe at the two white sofas with their jade-green cushions, and the low bleached oak coffee-table. 'It all looks brand-new,' she commented with approval.

'That's because it is.'

Rose raised her eyebrows. Heaven only knew how much he would be paying per month for a place like this. She asked the question she had been dreading asking. 'How long is the let for?'

There was a momentary pause. 'I am not renting it,' he said quietly. 'I bought it.'

'You *bought* it? What, just like that?' she asked incredulously, until she realised how preposterous she must have sounded. A place like this would be nothing to a man of Khalim's wealth.

He saw her look of discomfiture. 'And for security reasons, all the furniture had to be brand-new—'

'What, in case there was an explosive device stashed behind the sofa?' she joked, then wished she hadn't.

'Something like that,' he agreed wryly.

'Sorry. That was a stupid thing for me to say!'

He smiled. 'How very magnanimous of you, Rose.'

When he smiled like that she was utterly lost. 'So you've bought a house,' she observed slowly.

'Well, to be honest—nothing I looked at to rent—' he remembered the bemusement of house-owners when he'd turned up with his bodyguard in tow '—came up to—'

She met his glittering black gaze. 'Palace standards?' she questioned drily.

How he loved it when she teased him that way! 'Mmm.' He swallowed down the desire which had been bubbling over all week. 'Anyway,' he finished, 'it will be a good investment.'

A good investment. Of course. That was how the rich made themselves richer, wasn't it? They invested.

Trying not to feel a little like a commodity herself, Rose wandered over to one of the huge picture windows which overlooked an intensely green square surrounded by iron railings and looked out.

'A very good investment, I'm sure,' she echoed.

'My bodyguard will have the self-contained unit downstairs,' he explained, watching the sudden stiffening of her shoulders and wondering what had caused it. 'And the upper three storeys will be entirely for you…and for me.'

Rose swallowed down the excitement that his words had produced. For the past week—was it only a *week*? It had seemed like a century in passing—she had thought of nothing else. Tried to imagine the reality of sharing a flat with Khalim, and every time she had failed to make that final leap of faith. To think that they actually would. That he would arrange it all himself. And then bring her here to live with him. Because when she had suggested that she simply visit him on occasional evenings and stay the night, he had swiftly censured her suggestion with arrogant assertion.

'No!'

'No?'

His black eyes gleamed. She could fight him on this, but she would not win. Oh, no. 'I do not want you to bring cases of clothes here, or have one toothbrush here, and another at your flat. You will live here, Rose, with me.'

For how long? her heart wanted her to cry out, but she steeled herself against its plea. She probably only thought she loved him. Wanted him because he was so completely unattainable. She must not place emotional demands on him which he couldn't possibly meet, because in time it would wear down whatever it was they had between them.

And what was that?

'Rose?' He broke into her reverie with a silky question.

Well, now was the time of reckoning, she told herself as he drew her into his arms and lowered his dark, beautiful head to hers. Now they would be able to see what they had between them.

His kiss was fierce and hard and long, whipping her up into a frenzy of need which matched his.

He found himself wanting to rip the little sundress from her body, to lay her down on the floor and impale her there. But there had been little restraint in his physical dealings with her so far. Little desire to show her the mastery of which he was proud.

For he had learned his sexual skills well. His eighteenth birthday present from his cousin had been a trip to Paris, to a hotel which had been the last word in luxury. And there, awaiting him, had been his 'present'—a stunning redhead in her forties, with a body which most men only dreamed of. A woman of the world, of a certain age. And in the three days and nights which had followed, she had taught him everything there was to know about the act of love.

The most important being, she had purred with satisfaction, the ability to give a woman pleasure.

He looked down into Rose's milky-pale face, where her sapphire eyes shone out at him like bright stars, and he felt an unrecognisable kick of emotion. He wanted to pleasure his Rose, he realised. To give her more pleasure than she had ever dreamed of. He smiled with the heady anticipation of it.

'Come and let me show you the bedroom now.'

She took his proffered hand, feeling oddly shy as he took her into a white and blue bedroom which was dominated by a vast bed.

He was watching her carefully. 'Rose,' he said, almost gently. 'Why do you blush?'

She certainly wasn't going to tell him that his smile had made her feel almost like... She shook her head at the ridiculousness of it all. Like a virgin bride on her wedding night. Who the hell was she kidding?

Oh, I *wish*, she thought helplessly as he drew her into the circle of his arms. How I wish.

'Now.' His voice deepened as he ran his ebony gaze over her. 'At last.'

He undressed her slowly, and with infinite care, his fingers teasing and tantalising her as they unbuttoned the sundress and then peeled it from her body. And then, as though he had all the time in the world—off came her lacy brassière.

And finally, with his fingertips flicking light and teasing movements which thrilled her to the very core—he slowly removed her little lace panties.

'Now let me look at you,' he commanded softly.

She should have felt shy in her nakedness, when he still stood so formidably clad in his dark grey suit—but how could she feel anything but pride under that warm look of approval? Instinctively, she lifted her shoulders back and the movement emphasised the lush thrust of her breasts.

He felt the unmistakable wrench of desire. 'Get into bed,' he commanded softly. 'You're shivering.'

Shivering, yes—but her tremble had nothing whatsoever to do with the cold, but with the tingling sense of expectation which washed over her as he began to unknot his tie.

He unhurriedly slipped his jacket off, and hung it over the back of the chair.

Come on, she thought. Come *on*!

But if he read the hunger in her eyes he chose to ignore it, his dark gaze not leaving her face as he slowly began to unbutton his shirt.

The shirt joined the jacket on the chair, and he unbuckled his belt before unzipping his trousers.

'You could strip for a living,' she told him throatily, unable to keep her thoughts to herself any longer.

He smiled. 'So could you. What say we make a living of it together?'

It was an outrageous fantasy, tinged with a poignancy produced by that elusive word 'together'. But she lost the sadness as he climbed into bed to join her, and pulled her into his arms, his warm, living flesh making her feel on fire where they touched.

'Just you and me,' he murmured, and cupped her breast in his hand, feeling the nipple thrust and jut against his palm in instant reaction. 'How do you like that?'

'What—*that*?' She jerked her head jokingly towards her

breast, where his hand looked so shockingly dark against the whiteness of her skin.

But he shook his head, a rare kind of tenderness filling his voice. 'No,' he demurred. 'I meant the you and me bit.'

'Oh, that!' She was about to make a flippant comment, the kind of comment which would keep her safe from hurt. But she read in his eyes an elemental truth—that right at that moment he was holding nothing back from her. And didn't such a truth deserve another? 'Oh, that is a prize beyond rubies,' she told him huskily.

He groaned as his mouth replaced his hand, locking his lips hungrily against the rosy nub which sustained all life. He wondered if these breasts would ever suckle a child.

A child that could never be his!

'Rose,' he groaned again, and the slick lick of his tongue made her feel almost weak with longing, so weak that she gave into her most primitive desire and slid her hand down between the muscular thighs until she had found what she was looking for.

'Rose!'

Her wanton capture of him made him feel as weak as water in her hands. And so did the way she was touching him, her hands lightly caressing the rock-hard shaft of him. His eyes closed and his head fell back against the pillow. Never, since that first induction to the pleasures of the flesh, had he allowed a woman such freedom with his body.

'Stop, Rose,' he begged.

'You don't like it?' she asked him innocently.

'I like it.' He said a single word in Marabanese he hadn't realised he knew, and then gently closed his hand over hers to stop her. 'Too much.'

She realised how much she had enjoyed seeing him look as dreamily helpless as that. To see him fighting for control. It made her feel strong. *Equal.* 'Well, then?' she whispered close to his mouth, so close that he touched his lips to hers.

'This is intended to be traditional love-making, Rose,' he told her sternly.

'And no demonstration that I have a certain amount of experience—and that you aren't my first lover?'

There was no flippancy in her voice now, Khalim recognised—with a flash of insight which dispelled the black clouds of his jealousy. Nothing but a wistful trace of insecurity, as though he would be judging her and finding her wanting. He tipped her chin upwards, so that their eyes locked on a collision course.

'You push me far, Rose,' he told her. 'Sometimes too far, I think.'

'You went mad when you found out I was on the pill!'

He had to force himself to stay calm and drew a deep breath. 'My harsh words on the subject in Maraban were based on...jealousy,' he grated, spitting out the unfamiliar word. 'Jealousy that I was not your first lover—'

'And I was jealous that you weren't mine,' she said softly, filled with a sudden boldness—because what was to be gained by hiding the truth from him?

Khalim expelled a long, low breath, remembering the newness, the vitality and sheer power of their first encounter, and he sought to honour it in some way. 'I felt like your first,' he said.

'And I yours,' she whispered back.

'You are more my equal than any woman I have ever met, Rose. You live by different rules to the women in my country, and the life you have lived makes you the person you are today. And I like the person you are today.'

A person who could get him running halfway around London to find a place for them to live, much to Philip Caprice's bemusement and his bodyguard's outrage!

'So don't you like your women to be subservient?' she asked him teasingly, wondering what she had said that was so wrong, because his face darkened with a simmering look of bitterness.

He thought of the unknown woman who would one day become his wife. And his eyes flickered down to where Rose lay—so pale and so beautiful—her hair spread like a moonlit fan across his pillow.

He shook his head. 'I never want subservience from you, Rose,' he whispered. 'Never from you.'

And all her thoughts and doubts and questions were driven from her mind as he began to stroke her, as if she were some pampered feline, and she wrapped her arms around him, kissing his neck and the bare warm flesh of his shoulders.

Khalim found that he wanted to touch her for ever, to run his fingertips over the creamy satin of her skin, to explore her body until he knew every curve and every dip of it. It was a new sensation for him—the wish to prolong the waiting, until it reached such a fever-pitch that neither of them would be able to resist it.

'Khalim!' gasped Rose, as his skilful touch took her down erotic pathways she had never encountered before, so close to the edge that if he didn't... 'Khalim!'

'Mmm?' What exquisite pleasure it gave him to see his Rose lying there, her hips in frantic grind, powerless to resist him. The sight of a woman yielding to him had never before had the power to make his heart thunder as though it really *were* the very first time. He knew then that he could make her beg for him, and knew also that it would leave a bitter taste in his mouth. For he was as much in her thrall as she was in his. 'It is time,' he whispered against her hair.

He moved to lie above her, dark and dominant and utterly, utterly in control as he parted her thighs, smiling as he felt her honeyed moistness.

And he entered her not with the powerful thrust of that first time in the desert—as though he would die if he didn't join with her as swiftly as possible. No, this, thought Rose as an unstoppable warmth began to unfurl deep within her— this was a long, slow movement which seemed to pierce at the very heart of her.

They moved in conjunction, in perfect synchrony, her pale, curving flesh complementing the hard, lean lines of his. Each lingering thrust set her trembling, until her whole body seemed to shimmer with some unexpected light.

Khalim felt as though he were enveloped in some dark, erotic enchantment, and he had to use every once of self-restraint he possessed to hold back. Until he saw the sudden arching of her back, the inevitable stiffening and then indolent splaying of her limbs as rapture caught her in its silken net.

And only then did he let go, with a moan which seemed to be torn from his soul itself.

Only then did he shudder with the pleasure of fulfilment, until he came to a perfect stillness—and allowed his head to fall upon the cushioned splendour of her breast.

They dozed on and off for most of the afternoon, and then he made love to her again. And again. Until she sat up in bed with her blonde hair all tousled and falling in disarray around her shoulders, while he sucked erotically on her forefinger.

'Khalim?'

'Mmm?' He loved the salty-sweet taste of her skin.

'I'm hungry.'

'Hungry?' The thought of food had not occurred to him, not with such a feast here in his arms, but then he had taught himself to transcend hunger. When reaching puberty he had been sent into the desert with his tutor and taught to go without food for days. Existing on a little water and what few berries were available. It was the simple code of the desert: that you should learn to do without, because you never knew when you might need to.

'Yes, starving, actually!' complained Rose.

He released her finger and lay back on the pillow, the sheet rumpled by his ankles, his dark body gloriously and proudly naked. 'You want that we should ring out for some food?'

She opened her mouth to say yes, when she remembered,

and shut it again. They were trying to be ordinary, weren't they? And if they were an ordinary couple who had just moved into their first home, then they would certainly not have an excess of cash to throw about.

'No. Let's have something here,' she said and tossed her hair back over her shoulder. 'I brought a load of groceries with me, remember?'

Khalim shrugged, and gave a satisfied smile. 'Whatever you wish to prepare will taste like manna, Rose.'

She was about to get out of bed when she frowned at his easy assumption that *she* would cook. 'Why don't *you* make us something to eat, Khalim?'

'Me?' he questioned. *'Me?'*

'Yes, you! I'm not asking you to run naked up and down Park Lane—just make us a cup of tea and a sandwich!'

'A cup of tea and a sandwich,' he repeated, on a low growl, damned if he was going to admit to her that he hadn't ever had to prepare a meal for himself in his adult life! He swung his long legs out of bed and stood naked in front of her, a mocking question in the dark eyes as he saw her unconscious little pout. He put his hands low on his hips, in a gesture of pure provocation.

'Sure?'

Rose licked her lips. So he was trying to use his sexuality to get out of making her a sandwich, was he? What place equality now? 'Quite sure,' she answered primly, but immediately turned over to lie on her stomach so that he wouldn't see the sudden tightening of her breasts.

He returned after so long that Rose was certain he must have fallen asleep in the kitchen, carrying a loaded tray with him. And he still hadn't bothered to get dressed!

But to her surprise, the sandwich was creditable.

'That looks really good, Khalim!' she exclaimed.

He sizzled a look at her. 'Don't patronise me, Rose,' he warned.

'I wasn't!'

'Oh, yes, you were!' His eyes glittered. 'Just because I haven't had to fend for myself doesn't mean I don't know what to do, if I need to—and you wouldn't need to be a culinary genius to be able to cut off two slices of bread and wedge a little salad between them.'

Round one to Khalim, thought Rose with unwilling admiration as she bit into the most delicious sandwich she had ever eaten.

CHAPTER TWELVE

LIVING with a prince wasn't a bit as Rose had expected—though, when she stopped to think about it, what *had* she expected? It wasn't exactly the kind of situation where you could rummage through your life's memory box and come up with a comparable experience, was it?

But there was only one word she could use to describe it. Bliss. Sheer and utter bliss.

She had never lived with a man before—had never felt any desire to make such a commitment to anyone before Khalim—and she was amazed at the way they just kind of slotted together as though this had always been meant to happen.

To her astonishment, the same things made them laugh—though for all the wrong reasons. Television game shows and badly made sitcoms, for example. And corny jokes which Khalim had apparently never grown out of since his schooldays.

'It is enjoyable to have someone to share them with,' he murmured to her one morning, when she was about to leave for work.

She heard the trace of wistfulness in the deep timbre of his voice. 'What an isolated life you have led, Khalim!'

He shrugged. 'Of course. It goes with the territory.'

And the territory in his case was real, not imagined.

And the other aspect of their life which was as close to perfection as Rose could imagine was their love-life. Their *sex*-life, she corrected herself automatically.

Just because Khalim sometimes astonished her with amazing tenderness during the act of love, didn't mean that he actually *felt* love. Sex *was* sometimes tender, just as sometimes it was fast and furious, or deliciously drawn-out. In fact, it had a hundred different expressions, and Khalim seemed intent on exploring each and every one with her.

On the downside, there was no doubt that Khalim had been spoiled—both physically and spiritually. There was often a tussle as to who got their own way, with Khalim often expecting her to accede to *his* wishes, simply out of habit.

'No!' she protested one evening, when she walked into the kitchen to find that the breakfast cups and plates still hadn't been stacked in the dishwasher. 'It's *your* turn to sort out the kitchen, Khalim!'

Khalim's eyes narrowed. This was fast turning into the farce of a camping trip he had been forced to endure at school at the age of thirteen! 'Haven't we taken this living a normal life to the extreme?' he demanded fiercely. 'Surely even normal couples get someone in to do the housework!'

'Yes, they do,' said Rose patiently. 'But that doesn't include general tidying up, does it? And anyway—' she looked up at him in appeal '—isn't that more of the same of what you're used to? People waiting on you, so that you don't live in the real world at all?'

Khalim gave an impatient little snort. Didn't she realise that when she opened those great big baby-blue eyes at him like that, he would agree to almost anything? He walked over to where she stood, like some bright and glorious vision in a short white skirt and a clinging scarlet T-shirt, and pulled her into his arms.

'Khalim, no!'

'Say that like you mean it!'

'I do!' she said, half-heartedly.

He shook his head as he lifted her face to his. 'Oh, no, you don't, my beauty,' he murmured, and bent his lips to hers.

She responded to him the way she always responded— with complete and utter capitulation, opening her mouth greedily to the seeking warmth of his, and tangling her fingers luxuriantly in the thick, black hair.

He gave a groan as he cupped her T-shirted breast, thinking how he had longed to hold her in his arms like this all day. She was like a fever in his blood, a fever he must purge before too long. He *must*. 'Let's go to bed,' he demanded heatedly.

'No!'

'No?' His black eyes glittered. Why was she saying one thing, while her body was saying the precise opposite? 'You mean you want me to do it to you here, standing up?'

Rose felt the instant pooling of need. He was outrageous! Irrepressible! She loved him—oh, how she loved him. 'No,' she said again, and with an effort disentangled herself from his arms, knowing in her heart of hearts that she was going a little bit over the top about this. But for heaven's sake— there was a *principle* at stake here! 'Well, really I mean yes— but *not until after you've stacked the dishwasher*!'

'If you think I'm going to allow domesticity to start dominating the *important* things in life, then you have made a very poor judgement, Rose,' he'd said, with a silky and sexual threat, and kissed her again, very soundly.

She lost that particular battle—but the crazy thing was that she didn't particularly care. She didn't care about anything, she realised.

Except for her dark lover with the soul of a poet, who would never truly be hers.

They went out—of course they did—just like any other couple. Except that they were not—and excursions into the outside world brought that fact crashing home. For trips to restaurants or the theatre were always shadowed by the discreet but ever vigilant bodyguard, who was never more than a few steps away from Khalim. Several times they ate with Sabrina and Guy, and Rose found herself glancing at Sabrina's shiny new wedding band with more than a little envy.

And each morning they both left for work, just like any other couple.

'Do you *have* to go to work?' Khalim demanded sleepily from their bed one morning, when the thought of having her in his arms for the rest of the day was just too much to resist. Philip could deal with all the most urgent matters, he thought hungrily. He threw her a sizzling look. 'I mean, *really*?'

'I most certainly do!' she replied crisply, steeling herself against the promise in those night-dark eyes. 'Why, are you offering to "support" me from now on, Khalim?'

He smiled, knowing that her challenge was an empty one. That his feisty, independent Rose would sooner sweep the streets than accept money from him! 'Any time you like,' he mocked. 'Any time at all.'

And it said a lot about her emotional state for Rose to realise that the offer actually *tempted* her for a moment. She spent one heady moment thinking how wonderful it would be to be 'kept' by Khalim, before swiftly taking herself out of the flat and heading off for her offices in Maida Vale.

Each day, Khalim went to his suite at the Granchester to join Philip Caprice where he locked himself into matters of state affecting Maraban, settling down to study the papers which had been sent for his attention.

And lately there were more and more of them, he acknowledged as he began to accept that the burden of his inheritance began to creep ever closer.

The heady, pleasure-filled weeks crept stealthily by. Each night he received reports on his father's health, and the physicians assured him that he was weak, but stable.

But one evening he replaced the telephone receiver with a heavy hand, tension etching deep lines on the dark, beautiful face, and Rose's heart went out to him, even as a cold feeling of the inevitable crept over her. 'Don't you want to go out to see him?' she asked softly. 'Shouldn't you be there, with him?'

He met her troubled gaze, her foreboding echoed in his

own eyes as he saw their fantasy life coming to an end. He nodded. 'I shall go at the weekend,' he told her. 'Once I have concluded the American oil deal.'

Her heart began to pound as she heard something new in his voice. Something she would have preferred not to have heard. Distance. She had heard it once before in Maraban and it had frightened her then.

Distance.

She stumbled over the words. 'And you may...you may stay there, I suppose?'

There was a long pause. 'That depends—'

'Please be *honest* with me, Khalim! Otherwise what good will this whole...' she couldn't think of a single word which would sum up the magic of their weeks together, and so she plumped for the prosaic '...*affair* have been, if the truth deserts us when it really counts?'

'Affair?' he echoed thoughtfully and then nodded slowly. 'Yes. I may have to stay. And I won't be able to take you with me, you know, Rose.'

'I know that. I never expected you to.'

'No.' She had placed no demands on him whatsoever, apart from a stubborn determination for him to do his share of the household chores. Would it have made him happier if she had broken down? Wept? Begged him not to go, or to smuggle her back to some anonymous house in Maraban? Because that at least might have given him some indication of her true feelings for him.

Never before had he encountered a woman who didn't demand words of love and commitment—particularly in the aftermath of love-making. But Rose had not. Did she not want emotional reassurance from him, then? Or was her eminently practical side simply telling her that such words meant nothing. That actions were what counted—and that soon he would have to leave.

'Then we'd better make the last of these two days,' she said unhappily.

He nodded, wishing that he could take the sadness from her eyes. 'Let's start right now.' And he pulled her into his arms and kissed her, dazed by the emotional effect of that sad, sweet kiss. 'A kiss like there was no tomorrow,' he murmured.

I wish tomorrow never *would* come, thought Rose as she kissed him back with a hunger which verged on desperation, a desperation which grew into a storm of passion which left them shaking and helpless in its wake.

They were slavish in their attention to detail, to try to make their last hours together as perfect as possible. The meals they cooked were their favourite meals; the music they played the most poignant.

And their love-making took on an extra dimension—the sense of inevitable loss they both felt making it seem more profound than it had ever done before.

She played with his body as she would a violin, fine-tuning every single one of his senses until he would moan with helpless pleasure beneath her hands and her lips.

The night before he was due to leave, they ate a sensual supper in bed and she was just licking off the strawberry yogurt which she had trickled on the dark matt of hair which sprinkled his chest when the phone rang.

'Leave it to the machine,' he instructed, his eyes tight shut with the pleasure of what she had been doing with her tongue.

She shook her head and sat back on her heels, wearing nothing but an exquisite wisp of scarlet silk he had bought her and then fought to make her accept. 'It might be Maraban,' she whispered. 'It might be news of your father.'

Guilt evaporated his pleasure instantly and Khalim reached his hand out and snatched up the phone.

'Khalim!' he said.

As soon as he started speaking in rapid Marabanese, Rose knew that something was very wrong—even if the dark look of pain which contorted his features hadn't already warned her.

He spoke in an unfamiliar, fractured voice and nodded several times, and when he put the phone back down Rose knew without being told that the worst had happened.

'He is dead?' she asked, in a shaking voice.

He didn't answer for a moment, shaking his head instead. The inevitable. The expected. And yet no less hard to bear because of that.

'Yes, he is dead,' he answered, in a flat, toneless voice. 'He died unexpectedly an hour ago.'

'Khalim—' she went to put her hand out to him, but he had already swung his long, dark legs over the bed and begun to dress. 'Can I *do* anything? Do you want me to phone Philip?'

'Philip is already on his way over,' he said, still in that strange, flat voice. 'The plane is being fuelled—and we will leave for Maraban immediately.'

Rose bit her lip. 'I'm so sorry, Khalim.'

He turned then and she was shaken by the bleak look of emptiness on his face.

'Yes. Thank you.'

He looked forbidding, a stranger almost, but Rose didn't care. She couldn't stop herself from moving across the room and putting her arms around him in a warm gesture of comfort. His body felt stiff, as if it was trying to reject the reality of what he had just heard, but she hugged him all the tighter.

'I should have been there,' he told her brokenly. 'I should have *been* there!'

'You couldn't have known! You were planning to leave first thing! It was unexpected, Khalim. Fate!'

'Fate,' he echoed, and tightened his arms around her waist.

Let it go, she urged him silently. Let it *go*.

And maybe her unspoken plea communicated itself to him in some inexplicable way, for she heard him expel a long, tortured breath and then his arms came round her, his head falling onto her shoulder, and she felt his long, drawn-out shudder.

They stood like that for moments—minutes, aeons, perhaps—until the insistent jangling of the doorbell could be heard.

He raised his head to look at her, and there was the unmistakable glimmer of tears in the black eyes.

'Khalim?' she whispered.

The great black cloud of grief which was enveloping him lifted just for a moment as he met the soft sympathy in her eyes, and grief became momentarily guilt.

This was the moment, he realised. The moment of truth. He would have to let her go.

And he didn't want to.

'May the gods forgive me for saying this at such a time,' he whispered, knowing that there would never be another moment to say it, 'but I do not wish to lose you, Rose.'

Oh, the pain! The spearing, unremitting pain of imagining life without Khalim. 'It has to be.' How rehearsed the words sounded, but that was because they were. She had been practising a long time for this very moment. 'It *has* to be.'

The doorbell rang again.

He lifted her chin, sapphire light blinding from her eyes. 'I must be in Maraban,' he told her, and then he said very deliberately, 'but I can come back.'

She stared at him as hope stirred deep within her, even while logic told her that any hopes she harboured would be futile. 'How?' she whispered.

'When things are settled.' He shrugged his shoulders. 'I will be able to visit you from time to time. It won't be the same, but...' His words tailed off as he saw the frozen expression on her face.

'What, and become your English mistress, while you take a bride back in Maraban?'

'I have no bride in Maraban!' he grated.

'Not yet! But soon you will!' She let out a deep sigh.

'Having to be content with little bits of you, when I've had…had…' Only now her words tailed off, too. She had been about to say that she had had all of him, but that hadn't been true, had it?

She had had his company and his laughter and his body, but there had never been any mention from Khalim of the most important thing of all.

Love.

She shook her head, fighting to keep her dignity. He would remember her as his proud, independent Rose, not a snivelling wreck of a woman. 'No, Khalim,' she said firmly. 'It won't work.' She pictured a life where she would always be waiting. Waiting for the infrequent phone call. Waiting for news that he had taken a wife at last. News of his wedding. Or of his baby, perhaps… She shook her head as the pain lanced through her again.

'Better we end it now, Khalim. Cleanly and completely. At least that way we'll be left with our memories, instead of destroying what we once had.'

Had he really imagined that she would agree to his outrageous suggestion? Could he honestly see Rose resigning herself to a lifetime of playing the understudy? And yet he did not want to let her go. Damn her! He knew that she still wanted him, just as much as he wanted her—so why could she not just agree to his proposition?

His mouth tightened, and he removed her hands from where they lay locked upon his shoulders.

'And that is your last word on the subject?'

She met the anger in his eyes and she turned away rather than face it. She did not want her last memory of Khalim to be one of smouldering rage. 'Yes,' she said.

'So be it,' he said, with chilling finality. 'Philip is waiting.'

She heard him leave the room and go to answer the door, heard him speaking in an undertone to Philip, and then suddenly he was back and she whirled round to find him looking remote and frozen, and she guessed that reality really was beginning to kick in. She wanted to go up and comfort him again, but there was something so forbidding about the icy set of his features that she didn't dare.

She wondered if her face showed that inside her heart was breaking. 'Goodbye, Khalim.'

He thought how detached she looked, as if nothing could touch her. And perhaps nothing could—for *he* certainly could not. She wanted no part of him, unless she could have everything of him. She wanted too much! 'You will continue to live here?' he questioned.

'How can I?' She meant—how could she possibly stay in a place which had been filled with his presence if he was no longer there? How could she bear to face the empty space on the bed beside her? Or consign herself to being without his warm body enfolding hers night after night?

'The deeds of the house are in your name,' he said. 'I bought it for you.'

'And why did you do that?' she demanded. 'As a kind of insurance policy?'

'You have a way of reducing everything down to the lowest possible denominator, don't you, Rose?' he stormed. 'It was supposed to be an act of generosity—nothing more sinister than that!'

But suddenly she felt cheap. So this really *was* the payoff, was it? An expensive house in Chelsea to compensate for the fact that her sheikh lover had left her!

'I don't want your charity, Khalim!'

His face grew cold. 'Then please accept it as my gift, for that was the only way it was intended. Goodbye, Rose.' His black eyes raked over her one last time, before he turned away and out of the room without a backward glance.

Rose waited until she had heard the front door slam shut behind them and then counted slowly to a hundred, before she allowed herself the comfort of tears.

CHAPTER THIRTEEN

'ROSE, are you *mad*?'

Rose calmly finished placing the last of her clothes into a suitcase, and clicked the locks into place before looking up at Sabrina—a particularly glowing-looking Sabrina, she thought, with a brief pang of envy. But that was what being newly married did for you, wasn't it?

'No, I am certainly not mad. Why should I be?'

'Because this house is beautiful, and if Khalim wants you to have it—'

'I can't live here without him, Sabrina!' Rose thought how strained her voice sounded. Well, at least it would match the strain on her face. 'Can't you understand that?'

'I guess so.' Sabrina sighed. 'Guy was worried that something like this might happen.'

'You mean that Khalim would inevitably leave me to go back to Maraban and find someone more suitable?'

'Well, yes.' Sabrina bit her lip. 'I wanted to warn you about his reputation, but Guy said—'

'No.' Rose shook her head to interrupt her friend. 'I don't want Khalim portrayed as some feelingless heartbreaker who used me and then dumped me. I went into this with my eyes open, Sabrina. I knew exactly what would happen, and now it has.' And the pain of his leaving was more intense than she had imagined in her worst nightmares.

Sabrina had come straight round soon after Khalim had left for the airport. 'Khalim has just rung me,' she announced to a red-eyed Rose when she opened the door to her. 'Oh, darling Rose—I'm so very sorry.'

'He told you about his father, I suppose?' Rose questioned dully.

162

'Yes.' Sabrina shut the front door behind her. 'He also told me to look after you. He's worried about you, you know.'

'I'm not an invalid, Sabrina,' said Rose stiffly.

But actually, maybe she *was* beginning to feel like an invalid.

In the two hours since Khalim had left for the airport, she had wandered around the flat like a robot, picking up all her possessions and placing them in neat piles, ready to go.

It was surprising really, just how much of a home they had made. In three months of living together, they had built up much more than she remembered. Lots of books. Vases. A coffee set. A beautiful backgammon set. Little things she had brought to their home. A lump formed in the back of her throat and she swallowed it down.

No point in thinking like that. No point at all.

'But where will you *go*?' asked Sabrina.

Rose looked at her with a calm, frozen face. 'I'll be fine. Don't forget—I've still been paying the mortgage on my flat, all the time I've been living here with Khalim.'

'But I thought you said that Lara had moved that ghastly boyfriend of hers in.'

'Yes, she has.' Rose gave a worried frown, before a little of her customary fire returned to reassure her that she hadn't become a *complete* walking piece of misery. 'And she can jolly well move him out again!'

'And you're really going to sell this place?'

'Yes, I am.'

'Don't you think it's a little soon to be making major decisions like that?'

Rose shook her head. In a world which now seemed to have all the security of quicksand, there was only one thing she knew for sure. 'I won't change my mind,' she said quietly. 'I just know I have to go.'

'So will you buy somewhere else with the proceeds, if it's just the fact that you can't bear to live here without Khalim?'

'It isn't. I just don't want to be beholden to him in any way.'

'Oh, Rose, he can *afford* it!'

'That's not the point! I *know* he can afford it! But it will make me feel like it's some kind of pay-off.'

'I'm sure it isn't.'

'So I'm going to give the money to charity instead!' she declared.

'Khalim wouldn't want you to do that. He'd want you to use it on yourself. Guy says he's genuinely concerned about you—'

'Well, he needn't be,' said Rose stubbornly, because concern made her stupid heart leap with excitement. He might be *concerned*, but he wasn't here, was he? And he never would be, either. 'He's always telling me how brave and how strong I am. I'll get over it.'

Maybe if she said it often enough, she just might convince herself.

She stared at Sabrina's worried face. 'Khalim asked you out once, didn't he, Sabrina?'

Sabrina's eyes widened. 'Who on earth told you that?'

Rose smiled. 'Khalim did. He said…' Her voice began to waver as she remembered the closeness they had shared the night he had made the admission. 'He said that he didn't want there to be any secrets between us…' Her eyes filled with tears and she turned a stricken face to Sabrina who instantly came over and put her arms around her.

'Oh, Rose,' she whispered. 'Poor, darling Rose.'

'Just tell me one thing, Sabrina!' sobbed Rose helplessly. 'Why the hell did he have to be a *prince*? Why couldn't he have just been a normal *man*?'

The death of Khalim's father was announced on the national news that evening, and Rose found herself watching the set obsessively, unable to turn the television off, even though her sanity pleaded with her to.

There was a short clip showing Khalim arriving at Dar-gar airport, with hordes of people clogging up the tarmac and paying homage to their new leader.

How stern he looked, in his pure white robes, she thought longingly. And how icily and perfectly remote. Looking at the footage of his arrival, it seemed hard to believe that just a few hours ago they had been making love in the room next door.

She swallowed, and as the news switched to other items she turned the set off.

She went home to her flat that same evening, to find the place almost unrecognisable and Giles snoring on the sofa.

Biting back her temper, she marched over and shook him by the shoulder.

'Whoa!' He opened bleary eyes and blinked at her. 'Whassa matter?' he slurred.

Rose took a steadying breath as she backed off from the stench of stale alcohol. 'Where's Lara?'

'She's away filming. What are you doing here?'

'I'm moving back here—in to *my* home. I know it's short notice, but would you be able to find somewhere else to live, please, Giles? And if it's at all possible I'd like you out tonight.'

Giles sat up and sneered. 'What's happened? Has he kicked you out? Has your pretty prince tired of you?'

'Khalim's father died this morning,' she said, in a voice which was threatening to break.

Giles narrowed his eyes. 'So he's in charge now, is he? Wow!'

It shamed her that he had not expressed one single sentiment of sorrow for Khalim's father—even for convention's sake.

'Just go, will you, Giles?' she said tiredly.

'Okay, okay—I'll go and stay with my brother.'

Once he had gone, she set to cleaning the flat, and at least it gave her something to do to occupy herself, so that by midnight, when everything was looking pretty much normal again, she was able to take a long bath and fall into bed.

But she couldn't sleep.

For too long she had been used to drifting off in the warm haven of Khalim's arms. Now she felt cold. And alone. She put on a baggy T-shirt for comfort, but there was still precious little warmth to be found.

She found a purchaser for the house almost immediately. That part of Chelsea had people just *queuing* up to buy homes there—and she was lucky enough to find a newly engaged merchant banker who was a first-time buyer.

'I want to complete the sale as quickly as possible, that's my only condition,' she told him and his horse-faced fiancée.

'Soon as you like,' he agreed smoothly, barely able to contain his glee as he examined the luxurious wealth of fixtures and fittings.

Rose tried to throw herself into her work, and when the money for the sale came through she went straight to the Maraban Embassy in Central London. It was difficult to keep a rein on her emotions as she spoke to the receptionist—a man whose glittering black eyes reminded her of Khalim, and made her feel such a deep sadness.

'Yes?' he asked.

Rose pulled the cheque out of her handbag, still finding it difficult to come to terms with just how much money the house had made. Khalim had been correct, she thought wryly—it *had* been a good investment.

'I'd like to make a donation to the Maraban Orphans' Fund,' she said.

The receptionist put his pen down and his look of surprise quickly became a smile of pleasure. 'How very kind,' he murmured. 'I will ask one of our attachés to come down and speak with you.'

'Can't I just leave the money, and go?'

He glanced down at the cheque, narrowed his eyes in shock and shook his head. 'I'm afraid that will not be possible. You are extremely generous, Miss…' he glanced down at the cheque again '…Thomas.'

Twenty minutes later, Rose was shaking hands with a courteous if somewhat bland attaché, who kept thanking her over and over for her generosity.

'You would like to sign the book of condolence before you leave?' he asked.

Rose hesitated. 'Yes, please,' she said quietly.

They left her alone in a room where a black-draped photograph of Khalim's father hung above a simple arrangement of lilies, alongside which a single candle burned. It was a photo which must have been taken when he was in his prime. How like his son he looked with those stern, handsome features and those fathomless black eyes, she thought.

Hot tears stung her eyes as she lifted the pen and stared at it as if seeking inspiration. What to write?

And then the words seemed to come pouring out all by themselves.

'You were a fine ruler,' she wrote, 'whose people loved and respected you. May you rest in peace, in the knowledge that your only son has inherited your strength and your wisdom to take Maraban into the future.'

Somehow she got out of there without bursting into tears, but at least there was a sense of a burden having been lifted. She'd cut her ties with Khalim, she realised—and, in so doing, had shown her own strength and wisdom. Now she must get on with rebuilding her life.

But this was easier said than done.

A job which had once enthralled her now became a number of hours in the day to be endured. I *must* snap out of it, she told herself fiercely—or I won't have a job as well as my man.

Yet, try as she might, she found herself gazing sightlessly out of the window time after time.

In the weeks which followed Khalim's departure, images

came back to burn themselves in her mind's eye—and to haunt her with their poignant perfection.

She remembered the first time she had shared a bathtub with him, and after the inevitable love-making they had washed each other's backs, giggling as bubbles frothed up and slid over the side and onto the floor.

He had looked at her with an expression of mock-horror. 'Now who is going to clean *that* up?'

'You are! You're the one who insisted on joining me in the bath!'

In that split-second of a moment Khalim had looked care-free—his rare and beautiful smile making her heart race. 'You'll have to make me, Rose!'

'I have my methods,' she had purred boastfully, her hands sliding underneath the water to capture him, and he had closed his eyes in helpless pleasure.

So what was she doing remembering *that*? Trying to torture herself? To remind herself of how unexpectedly *easy* it had been to adjust to a man like Khalim? And it had.

She hadn't expected to be able to sit enjoying such simple companionship with him in the evenings as they'd played backgammon or cooked a meal together. Oh, *why* had it been so easy? she asked herself in despair.

And then, two nights later, she had a visitor when she arrived back at the flat after work.

Philip Caprice was sitting in a long, dark limousine outside the flat and Rose's heart leapt when she saw the car, her eyes screwing up in an attempt to scan the smoky glass, in futile search for the one person she really wanted to see.

Philip must have seen her approaching, because by the time she came alongside the car he had got out and was standing waiting, a polite but slightly wary smile on his face.

'Hello, Rose,' he said.

She nodded in greeting. His eyes looked very green against his lightly tanned skin. Tanned by the glorious heat of the Maraban sun, she observed with a pang. 'Philip,' she gulped.

'May I come inside and talk to you?'

She wanted to say no, to ask him what was the point—but her curiosity got the better of her. And, besides, she wanted to hear news of Khalim.

'Yes, of course you can.'

'Thank you.'

Lara was still away filming and so the flat was empty and mercifully tidy and she found herself thinking about the time when she had turned up with Khalim to find total chaos. Remembered the rather fastidious look of horror which had darkened his handsome face, and the resulting decision for him to find them somewhere to live.

Just *stop* remembering, she told herself fiercely. Stop it!

'Would you like some coffee, Philip? Or tea, perhaps?'

He shook his dark head. 'Thank you, but no.'

He seemed, she thought, a trifle uncomfortable. What was the purpose of his visit? she wondered. 'What can I do for you, Philip?' she asked pleasantly.

'Khalim has sent me.'

She bit her lip. 'H-how is he?'

'He's sad, of course—but coping magnificently, just as you would expect.'

'Yes.' Of course he was. Swallowing down her pain, she said, 'So what is the purpose of your visit here today, Philip?'

Philip nodded thoughtfully, as if her reaction was not the one he would have anticipated. 'He asked me to bring you this.' He opened up his briefcase and withdrew a slim, dark leather box and handed it to her.

Rose stared down at it. 'What is it?'

'Why don't you open it, and see?'

Caution told her to give it straight back to him, but that old devil called curiosity seemed to be guiding her actions instead. With miraculously unshaking hands, she opened the clasp.

Inside was a necklace, although the word seemed oddly

inadequate for the magnificent piece of jewellery which dazzled at her from its navy-velveted backdrop.

A necklace of sapphires and diamonds which blazed with unmatchable brilliance, and, at the very centre of the piece, a single deeper blue sapphire, the size of a large walnut.

Rose lifted her eyes to his, her face pale and her voice now trembling. 'Wh-what is the p-purpose of this?'

'Isn't it obvious?'

'Not to me it isn't, no. Why is he sending his emissary with expensive baubles? To sweeten me up? Is that it? To induce me to fall in with his wishes?'

'He doesn't want it to be over, Rose.'

'Well, it *is* over,' she said stubbornly. 'It has to be. I thought I made that clear. I'm not prepared to become his part-time mistress, Philip—I told him that unequivocally. So perhaps you'd like to give this back to him, and tell him that pieces of jewellery, no matter how gorgeous, will not change my mind.' And she snapped back the clasp and handed it back to him.

Philip stared down at the proffered case for a long moment before he took it. 'You won't change your mind?' he asked slowly.

She shook her head, but with the pain again came the sense of liberation, and of dignity. 'I can't. Tell him that. And tell him not to contact me again—that's best for both our sakes.' She kept her voice steady. 'Tell him to make a happy life for himself in Maraban, and I will endeavour to do the same for myself in England.'

Philip nodded. 'He will not be pleased.'

'I didn't imagine for a moment that he would be. And please tell him not to mistake my resistance for enticement.' She gave a heavy sigh. 'I'm trying to be practical, Philip, for both our sakes.' And my heart is too fragile. If I stop it now, I will survive, she thought. And so will he. If I let it continue in the cloak-and-dagger way of being his foreign mistress, then I risk it breaking into a thousand pieces.

'Do you have any message for him?'

She longed to ask Philip to tell him that she loved him, and that she would never stop loving him—but wouldn't that give him the power to try and wear her down? And who knew how long she would be able to resist *that*?

She nodded. 'Just wish him luck, Philip. Tell him to make Maraban great.'

Philip looked as though he wanted to say something else, but clearly thought better of it. He dropped the case into his briefcase and gave a brief, courteous smile.

'That was never in any doubt,' he said. 'It is his personal happiness which is precarious.'

So he wanted it all. A wife in Maraban and a mistress in London. She remembered something that Khalim had once said to her, and shrugged. 'And that, I'm afraid, Philip—that goes with the territory.'

CHAPTER FOURTEEN

THERE were swathes of dark green holly leaves, their blood-coloured berries gleaming as Rose looped them through the bannister of the sweeping staircase which dominated the hallway of her parents' farmhouse.

'There!' She stood back to admire her handiwork and turned to where her brother was standing holding all the pins and tacks. 'What do you think, Jamie?'

'Perfect,' smiled her brother.

'And you like the tree?'

He stared for a moment at the huge conifer which stood next to the hatstand. She had festooned it with silver and gold baubles and tied scarlet ribbons around the ends of all the branches. 'Perfect,' he said again, and narrowed his eyes thoughtfully at her. 'You seem happier these days, Rose.'

She hesitated for a moment. Did she? Then appearances could be very deceptive. Because even though most of the time she *did* feel, if not exactly happy, then certainly more contented than before—the pain of losing Khalim could still come back to haunt her and tear at her heart with an intensity which had the power to make her feel weak and shaking.

She shrugged. 'Well, it's been over a year now since...' Her voice tailed off. To say the words made it real, and so much of her wished that it were nothing but some cruel fantasy.

'Since lover-boy went back to Maraban?'

She frowned. 'There's no need to say it in quite that tone, Jamie.'

'What way is that? The disapproving way in which any brother would speak if their sister had had her heart broken by a man who should have known better?'

172

Rose sighed. 'I keep telling you—he didn't exactly have to kidnap me! I knew exactly what I was getting into, I just—'

'Expected that the end result might be different?' he prompted softly.

Well, no. Of course she hadn't, not really. She had *hoped*, of course she had—because hope was part of the human condition, even when deep down you knew that to hope was useless.

She shook her head. 'I gave up hoping a long time ago, Jamie. Let's leave it, shall we? What time are Mum and Dad getting back?'

'Their train gets in at three, and I said I'd go and collect them from the station. Though it beats me why anyone in their right mind should choose to go Christmas shopping in London, on Christmas *Eve*!'

Rose smiled. 'It's a family tradition, remember? And I like traditions! Now I think I'll go and hang some greenery round the fireplace. Want to help me?'

Jamie grinned. 'I think I'm all spent out where decorating activities are concerned! I might just go and put a light under that pot of soup. Going to have some with me, Rosie?'

'No, thanks. I had a late breakfast.'

'You are eating properly again now, aren't you?'

'I never stopped!'

'That's why when you turn sideways you could disappear?'

She forced a smile. 'I'm not *thin*, Jamie—just slimmer than I used to be.'

'Hmm. Well, Mum is planning to feed you up on Christmas pudding—be warned!'

'Can't wait!'

She went into the sitting room and sat down on the floor to begin tying together the greenery she had brought in from the garden.

Hard to believe that they would soon be into a new year,

but maybe the brand-new start would give her the impetus she needed to get on with her life. *Really* get on with her life.

She had made changes. Had switched from Headliners to another, smaller agency—where the different faces and different clients had forced her to concentrate on work, instead of dwelling on the darkly handsome face she missed with such an intensity.

And she had sold her flat in Notting Hill, too. She had bought somewhere slightly smaller and in a less fashionable area of London, which meant that she no longer needed to take in a lodger.

She didn't have to pretend to be feeling good in front of a flatmate now that she lived on her own. And if she felt like a quiet evening in, reading or watching television, then there was no one to nag her about going out and *meeting* people. She didn't want to meet people. Especially not men. She had known very early on that Khalim would be an impossible act to follow, and in that her instincts had not failed her.

Somewhere in the distance, she heard the chiming of the doorbell, and because she was up to her ears in stray bits of conifer she hoped that Jamie might answer it. She heard the door open, and then murmurings.

'Rose!'

She blinked at the rather urgent quality in Jamie's voice. 'What is it?'

'You have a visitor.'

She looked up to see Jamie framed in the doorway of the sitting room, his face white and tense, a look of something approaching anger hardening his mouth.

'What's the matter?' she asked.

'It's *him*!'

'What is?' she questioned stupidly.

'*Khalim!*' he whispered. 'He's here. Right now. Waiting in the hall.'

The world span out of control and she felt all the blood

drain from her face. 'What does he want?' she whispered back, in a voice which did not sound like her own.

'To see you, of course!' Jamie glowered. 'You don't *have* to see him, you know, Rose! I can send him away, if that's what you want.'

And wouldn't that be best?

She had done everything in her power to eradicate him from her memory in the intervening year since she had last seen him. She had been largely unsuccessful in this, it was true, but it hadn't been through a lack of trying. Wouldn't seeing him again just reopen all those old wounds, making the original injury even worse than before?

But how could she *not* see him—when her heart was banging fit to burst at the thought that he was here? Now.

She stood up and brushed some spray fronds of greenery from the front of her jeans. 'No, I'll see him, Jamie,' she said quietly. 'Will you send him in, please?'

In an effort to compose herself, she walked over to the window and looked out at the stark winter landscape which seemed to mirror the icy desolation of her emotional state.

She heard him enter the room. That unmistakable footfall.

'Rose?' came the deep and slightly stern entreaty from behind her.

Heart hammering, Rose forced herself to face him, and when she did her breath caught in her throat with longing.

He looked...

Oh, but he looked perfect—more perfect than any man had a right to look. And he was not wearing one of the immaculate suits he usually wore when he was in Europe—instead, he was dressed in the flowing, silken robes of Maraban. The ebony eyes were gleaming with some unspoken message and his face was as stern and as fierce as she had ever seen it.

Sabrina's heart turned over with love and longing as she stared into the unfathomable glitter of his eyes, but she prayed that her face didn't register her feelings.

Why was he here?

'Hello, Khalim,' she said, in a voice which she didn't quite recognise as her own.

He thought how pale her face was, so that the blue eyes seemed to dominate its heart-shaped frame with their unforgettable dazzle. And how fragile she looked, too—the jeans he remembered looking slightly loose on the waist, and around the swell of her bottom. 'Hello, Rose,' he said softly.

She drew a deep breath. 'How did you find me?'

He gave a brief, hard smile. It had been clear that she had not wanted him to find her. She had changed her job and changed her flat—no, the message to stay away had been quite clear. 'It was not difficult.' He shrugged.

Not for him, no—of course it wasn't. 'Did you get Philip to search for me?' she mocked.

'What did you expect me to do?' he retorted. 'Scour the pages of the telephone directory myself? Running a country takes up almost all of my waking hours, Rose.'

'Of course. I shouldn't have been so flippant.' Her voice trembled. 'H-how is Maraban?'

'Lonely,' he said with the brutal honesty which seemed to come so easily around her.

She quashed the foolish flare of hope which leapt in her heart. She had never allowed fantasy to get in the way of reality where he was concerned, and she wasn't about to start now. 'Oh? So no suitable bride been found for you yet?'

'No,' he agreed equably, because the waspish way she asked that question told him that maybe her message of wanting him to stay away had been ambivalent. That maybe she still cared. 'No wife.'

'But not through lack of trying, I imagine?'

He was not going to tell her lies, nor to play games with her. 'That's right.' He allowed his mind to briefly dwell on every available high-born Maraban woman who had been brought before his critical eye. And how every doe-eyed look of submission had only emphasised the equality he had shared with Rose.

'But none of them came up to your exacting standards, Khalim?'

'Not one.' He smiled. 'That's why I'm here today.'

She reminded herself of what his terms had been before he'd left, and they would not have changed—why should they when the circumstances were exactly the same as before?

'Would you mind making yourself a little clearer?'

He owed her this. The unadorned truth. The only words which would express the only thing which mattered.

'I love you, Rose.'

The words rang in her ears. Alien words. Secretly longed-for but inconceivable words…words from which she would never recover if they weren't true. She met the lancing black stare and her heart began to pound. Because it didn't matter what logic or common sense told her—Khalim would not use words like that if he didn't mean them. Why would he?

Khalim narrowed his eyes as he watched the wary assessment which had caused a frown to appear between the two delicate arches of her eyebrows. Had he imagined that she would fall straight into his arms the moment that those words were out of his mouth?

'Shall I say it again?' he questioned softly. 'That I love you, Rose. I have always loved you. I shall love you for the rest of my days, and maybe beyond that, too.'

She shook her head distractedly. It didn't matter—because fundamentally nothing had changed. 'I can't do it, Khalim,' she whispered. 'I just can't do it.'

Black brows knitted together. 'Do what?'

'I can't be your mistress—I just can't—because it will break my heart.' Maybe if she appealed to his innate sense of decency, he might go away and leave her alone. Stop tempting her into breaking every rule in the book. She sucked in a huge, shuddering breath. 'You see, I love you, too—I love you in a way I didn't think it was possible to love.'

'And that's a problem, is it?' he asked gently.

'Of course it's a problem! I can't say I'm not tempted to become your mistress—of course I am! I've ached and ached for you since you went back to Maraban, and just when I thought I might be getting over it—'

'*Are* you?' he questioned sternly. 'Getting over me?'

The truth was much more important than remembering not to pander to his ego. 'No, of course I'm not,' she admitted. And she didn't think she ever would. 'But what chance do I have if we become lovers again? I'll just get sucked in, deeper and deeper, and then sooner or later there *will* be a Maraban woman who you will want to make your wife—'

'Never!' he said flatly.

'You can't say that!'

'Oh, yes, I can,' he corrected resolutely. 'There is only one woman who I could ever imagine making my wife. One woman who I have every intention of making my wife, and that woman is you, Rose. It only ever *has* been you.'

She stared at him in disbelief, telling herself that she had not heard him properly. Words of love and commitment she had only ever listened to in her wildest dreams. And dreams didn't come true—everybody knew that. 'You can't mean that.'

He smiled then as he heard the loving tremble in her voice. 'Yes, I can, Rose. I have the agreement of my government to make you my bride just as soon as the wedding can be arranged.'

She longed to touch him, to run her fingertips with reverent wonder along the sculpted perfection of his face, but she was scared. 'But why the change of heart?'

He shook his head. 'No change of heart, my darling—that has remained constant since the first time I ever laid eyes on you. The difference is that my advisors have come to realise that a happy man makes a good ruler.' The stark, beautiful truth shone like ebony fire from his eyes. 'And I cannot ever be a happy man without you by my side. Come to me, Rose, come and kiss me, and make my world real once more.'

She didn't need to be asked twice—she was across the room and in his arms, and as he buried his lips in the flaxen satin of her hair she discovered that he was shaking as much as she was.

'Khalim,' she said brokenly.

'Sweet, sweet, beautiful Rose—my Rose, my only Rose,' he murmured against its scented sweetness, and she raised her face to his in wonder as she read the look of love on his face.

He bent his head to kiss her, and an intense feeling of emotion threatened to rock the very foundations of his world.

They were breathless when the kiss ended, and Rose lifted her hand up, traced the sensual outline of his lips with her finger.

'They don't mind? They honestly don't mind you taking a Western woman for your bride?'

His shrug was rueful. 'The more traditional element of the court were distinctly unimpressed, but the hand of my father guided events—even beyond his death.'

'I don't understand.'

'Do you remember he asked to meet you?'

'Yes, of course I do!'

'He had sensed my distraction since meeting you and wanted to know why. And when he met you, he understood perfectly.' He paused. 'Afterwards he commented on your similarity to my great-great-grandfather's true love.'

'Y-yes,' she said slowly as she waited for the rest of the story to unfold.

'And Malik was never the same man after she was sent away—'

'Is that Malik the Magnificent?' she asked tentatively.

Khalim narrowed his eyes. 'How on earth did you know that, Rose?'

'I read about it, of course—in the chapter about your ancestors.'

He smiled, thinking that she would make a wonderful

Princess of Maraban! 'His heart was not into ruling after that. He complied with convention and took a Marabanesh wife, but was left a bitter and empty shell of a man.' His eyes met hers with a candid light. 'My father did not want to see history repeating itself.'

'History or destiny?' she echoed softly, and her eyes lit up with a glorious sense of the inevitable. 'Or maybe even *pre*-destination, as though all this was somehow *supposed* to happen all along.'

'Predestination?' His deep voice lingered thoughtfully on the word, and he nodded. 'Yes. It exists. It's what drives us all. It's why I met you, Rose.'

The love from his eyes dazzled her, and she gazed up at him. 'What on earth can I say to something as beautiful as that?' she whispered.

He smiled. 'Say nothing, sweet Rose. Just kiss me instead.'

EPILOGUE

THE late afternoon air was warm and scented as Rose and Khalim alighted from the smoky-windowed car and made their way towards their apartments—situated in the grandest part of the palace. And where once she had been taken to see Khalim's father as he lay dying.

Rose was grateful to have met him, no matter that the visit had been brief. It pleased and warmed her to know that he had had the perception and the wisdom to override convention and to let their wedding take place.

And what a wedding!

The whole of Maraban had gone absolutely wild with excitement, happy that their leader should have found a woman to love at last, and proud of the pale, blonde beauty of his Rose.

Guy had been delighted to be best man, and Sabrina her maid of honour, and all of Rose's family had been flown out to Maraban in some style. They had feasted and celebrated for three enchanting days, crushing lavender and rose petals beneath their feet as they danced, and at the very end of the celebrations Rose and Khalim had ridden through Dar-gar on their Akhal-Teke horses. Rose's mount in a pure white—as white as the winter snows—and in such contrast to Khalim's Purr-Mahl.

For he had insisted that she learn to ride—had even insisted on teaching her himself. And what a hard taskmaster he had proved to be—not satisfied until she could gallop alongside him with a fearlessness which matched his own.

Never satisfied...and yet always satisfied.

It was the same in their marital bed on silken sheets which whispered and wrapped themselves around their entwined bodies. Would their passion for each other never abate? she sometimes asked herself in helpless wonder as she came back down to earth from some remote place of pleasure which Khalim had taken her to.

She hoped not.

He touched a light hand to her elbow as a golden shaft of sunlight turned her hair to pure spun gold. 'Tired?' he asked softly, thinking how all the people had warmed to her that afternoon. As they always warmed to her. For his Rose had a gentle understanding which made people instantly love her.

As he loved her, he thought fiercely—loved her more than he would have thought possible to love another person.

'Tired?' Rose smiled up at him dreamily. 'No, of course I'm not. It was a wonderful afternoon. Wasn't it?' she asked him, a touch anxiously.

'You know it was.' They had been to the opening of the newly refurbished Maraban Orphanage, now named after its princess. No announcement had ever been officially made, but word had got around on the grapevine of Rose's generous donation when she'd still been living in London, when she had believed her relationship with Khalim to be over.

'Such unselfishness,' his mother had cooed, totally in thrall with her daughter-in-law herself. As were his sisters. In fact, everyone. Well, almost everyone.

Khalim allowed a wistful smile to play at the corners of his mouth.

Except for Philip, of course. Philip had tendered his resignation a year after Rose had become Princess, even though both she and Khalim had asked him to reconsider.

But Philip had shaken his dark, handsome head, the green eyes enigmatic, giving little away.

'I cannot,' he had demurred.

'It isn't *me*, is it, Philip?' Rose had asked him.

He gave her a fond smile. 'Never you, Princess,' he had murmured. 'But I am part of the past, it is time for me to go. Your new emissary must be someone who will engage in your joint future. Think about it. You know that what I say is true.'

Yes, Khalim had known—Philip's insight had been one of the reasons he had made him his emissary. And even Rose had known that, too—though she was sad for a little time, because she herself had become fond of the cool Englishman and his connection with her old life.

The doors to their apartments were opened and they went inside, Khalim giving a swift shake of his dark head to the robed figure who looked enquiringly at him. He wanted to be alone with her.

Because Rose had seen very early on in her marriage that absolutely everyone wanted a piece of Khalim, and that unless she put her foot down their time together would be limited indeed. And so—to much outrage at first—she had insisted on having their own kitchen built inside their private apartments.

'I don't always want to be served food,' she had told Khalim stubbornly when he'd tried to oppose her plan. 'Sometimes I want to cook myself, for just the two of us, the way I used to when we lived together in London, remember?'

He'd smiled. 'How could I ever forget?'

'And, of course, for you to cook for *me*!' She had seen his look of outrage and slanted him a provocative smile. 'We don't want you forgetting how to fend for yourself, do we, my darling?'

'Oh, Rose,' he had moaned, helpless in the capture of that smile.

He watched her now as she moved with such elegant grace towards the kitchen, and followed her, wondering whether he should take her to bed now, or later. That was the trouble and also the joy of their relationship—he never stopped wanting her. But his powers of self-control had been sorely tested.

Today, her flaxen hair was complimented by the lavender silk of the gown she wore, and he looked at her with a slightly jealous pride. Too bad that they were now having to contend with hordes of foreign journalists eager to capture the beauty of the Marabanesh princess. His Rose was going international, while he wanted her all to himself! And yet deep in his heart he knew that she gave herself completely to him. And always would.

She turned to find him watching her and thought that right now was just the moment to make her gift to him. 'Khalim,' she said softly, in perfect Marabanese. 'Shall I make some mint tea for us to drink?' And she thought that she would never forget the look on his face as he stared at her with a kind of dawning wonder.

'Rose?'

She continued speaking in his native tongue. 'I've been having lessons,' she told him shyly. 'From Fatima. Whenever you've been dealing with affairs of state, I've been poring over my dictionary! And Fatima says I'm almost fluent and that I—'

But she couldn't say any more on the subject, because he had swiftly crossed the room, and had pulled her into his arms and was looking down at her with a fierce and tender love.

'Were the gods looking down on us the day I met you, Rose?' he demanded heatedly. 'And were they Jupiter and Venus?'

'I expect so,' she said demurely, because she knew just what he wanted when he looked at her like *that*. What *she* wanted, too, more than anything else.

She gave herself up to his kiss. Well, the mint tea could always wait.

MILLS & BOON®

Makes any time special™

Mills & Boon publish 29 new titles every month. Select from...

Modern Romance™   Tender Romance™

Sensual Romance™

Medical Romance™   Historical Romance™

MAT2

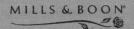

MILLS & BOON®

Modern Romance™

DUARTE'S CHILD by Lynne Graham

Only days before she gave birth, Emily left her husband, Duarte de Monteiro. Now Duarte has traced her and his baby son, and brought them back to Portugal. But has he done so because he loves her, or just because he wants his son?

THE UNFORGETTABLE HUSBAND by Michelle Reid

For a year Samantha had been existing with amnesia, but when a dark, imposing man walked into her life, she knew her past was about to be revealed. Andre Visconte insisted he was her husband. But why hadn't he found her until now?

THE HOT-BLOODED GROOM by Emma Darcy

When Bryce Templar met Sunny at a conference the attraction between them was like a bolt of electricity. He wanted Sunny, and needed an heir—but would there be more to their marriage than a baby bargain?

THE PROSPECTIVE WIFE by Kim Lawrence

Matt Devlin is the ultimate millionaire playboy. His family are constantly trying to find him a wife, so he is instantly suspicious when blonde, beautiful Kat turns up as his physiotherapist! The attraction is instantaneous…

On sale 3rd August 2001

Available at most branches of WH Smith, Tesco, Martins, Borders, Easons, Sainsbury, Woolworth and most good paperback bookshops

MILLS & BOON®

Modern Romance™

RESTLESS NIGHTS by *Catherine George*

Gabriel is a girl of independence, happy with her career in London. But when Adam Dysart strides back into her life, his charisma turns her balanced emotions to jelly! Gabriel knows if she lets him into her life, she'll let him into her bed too...

THE ALVARES BRIDE by *Sandra Marton*

No one knew the father of Carin's baby—but during the birth she called out a name: Raphael Alvares! The powerful Brazilian millionaire rushed to Carin's bedside—but had he only come because pride forced him?

MERGER BY MATRIMONY by *Cathy Williams*

Destiny has inherited a business worth millions! But her company is desired by a predator: handsome, ruthless tycoon Callum Ross. He's determined to buy; she won't sell. So he has a proposal for her—merger by matrimony!

AN ELIGIBLE STRANGER by *Tracy Sinclair*

Nicole Trent would never hand over her orphaned nephew to his father's cold-hearted brother. Yet how could she deny him the privileged lifestyle to which he was entitled? Swept off to Philippe Galantoire's chateau in France, Nicole careered headlong into a world of forbidden desire...

On sale 3rd August 2001

Available at most branches of WH Smith, Tesco, Martins, Borders, Easons, Sainsbury, Woolworth and most good paperback bookshops

0701/01b

A Perfect Family

An enthralling family saga by bestselling author

PENNY JORDAN

Published 20th July

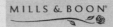

4 FREE
books and a surprise gift!

We would like to take this opportunity to thank you for reading this Mills & Boon® book by offering you the chance to take FOUR more specially selected titles from the Modern Romance™ series absolutely FREE! We're also making this offer to introduce you to the benefits of the Reader Service™—

★ FREE home delivery
★ FREE gifts and competitions
★ FREE monthly Newsletter
★ Exclusive Reader Service discounts
★ Books available before they're in the shops

Accepting these FREE books and gift places you under no obligation to buy, you may cancel at any time, even after receiving your free shipment. Simply complete your details below and return the entire page to the address below. *You don't even need a stamp!*

YES! Please send me 4 free Modern Romance books and a surprise gift. I understand that unless you hear from me, I will receive 6 superb new titles every month for just £2.49 each, postage and packing free. I am under no obligation to purchase any books and may cancel my subscription at any time. The free books and gift will be mine to keep in any case.

P1ZEA

Ms/Mrs/Miss/Mr ....Initials..................................
                                                                    BLOCK CAPITALS PLEASE
Surname ....
Address ....

....

....Postcode.................................

Send this whole page to:
UK: FREEPOST CN81, Croydon, CR9 3WZ
EIRE: PO Box 4546, Kilcock, County Kildare (stamp required)